S0-BIR-394

THE
HERMIT
OF
DOGWOOD

THE
HERMIT
OF
DOGWOOD

A NOVEL BY

CALVIN R. EDGERTON

Pleasant Word

© 2006 by Calvin R. Edgerton. All rights reserved.

Pleasant Word (a division of WinePress Publishing, PO Box 428, Enumclaw, WA 98022) functions only as book publisher. As such, the ultimate design, content, editorial accuracy, and views expressed or implied in this work are those of the author.

No part of this publication may be reproduced, stored in a retrieval system or transmitted in any way by any means—electronic, mechanical, photocopy, recording or otherwise—without the prior permission of the copyright holder, except as provided by USA copyright law.

The Hermit of Dogwood is a work of fiction. All characters, situations, and places are products of the author's imagination.

A Publication of Simple Press™ in cooperation with Pleasant Word, a Division of Winepress Publishing.

Keep Me Simple, Lord, lyrics ©2006 by Calvin R. Edgerton.

Please visit the author's website at calvinedgerton.com.

ISBN 1-4141-0728-5
Library of Congress Catalog Card Number: 2006905361

Chatham County Libraries
500 N. 2nd Avenue
Siler City, North Carolina 27344

Dedicated to
Rebecca, Hinton,
and Georgia Kate,
and to Dotty,
without whom none of this
would be possible

"A town has a nervous system and a head and shoulders and feet...and a town has a whole emotion."

—John Steinbeck
The Pearl

"And by him we cry, 'Abba, Father.' The Spirit Himself testifies with our spirit that we are God's children."

—Paul of Tarsus
(Romans 8:15)

CHAPTER 1

Mary Della Johnson discovered her carving on the tenth day of her mourning. She pulled into her driveway just as the sun's bright orange beams began their slide toward the other side of the world.

Since the death of her young son more than a week earlier, she had felt it a hard-won victory simply to get out of bed in the morning. But today she had been determined to rise as soon as her eyes took in the light of day, to get ready for work, to go to work, to have a normal day.

She had prayed the night before for the courage to do this one simple thing, and now she had done it. She considered this a miracle, and she gave the

Lord a silent nod of praise as she walked across the soft grass to her front door.

She slid the dull brass key into the lock and delighted in the setting sun's reflection on the small window in the door panel. She took a cautious step backward when she saw a small bundle of cloth tucked neatly onto the threshold. She did not know what to make of the bundle, but she did not hesitate to pick it up, carry it to her table and lay it out.

Wrapped inside the cloth was an angel, carved in wood.

In the angel's arms was a small child, smiling, reaching its arms toward the angel's face. Mary Della took a sudden deep breath when she realized that the young child in the angel's arms bore a strong resemblance to her son, Marty.

On a foggy Monday morning Marty had bounced out of the house and down the paved walkway to the street. He joined two other children at the curb. They waited for the bus and Mary Della watched from the porch. The bus stopped and her son turned to wave goodbye to his mother. Then, he stepped off the curb and into the path of a speeding garbage truck. In a wink of time that had seemed to Mary Della like an eternity, Marty was gone.

Now, in the sweet details of the face of the boy carved in wood, she saw the bright eyes of her young son. She cried, and then calm like still water enveloped her and she knew immediately that Marty was with Jesus. She did not know from which part of heaven this certainty came, but it was there all the same. This artfully-carved angel brought to her soul an assurance unlike any she'd known.

She fell to her knees and thanked God for this wonderful gift. Her tears fell onto the face of the child and she hugged the carving close to her chest. She placed the carving on her fireplace mantle and sat in a dining chair and gazed at it for a long time. And she wondered who would give her such an extraordinary thing.

"It was like a slap in the face. I can still feel the sting."

Marvin Wilkins had asked Pastor Robbins to join him for lunch. The pastor was the only person to which he could confide his deepest thoughts.

"I came home from work like I'd done every working night for six years," he said. "I opened the front door, expecting to see Jo in the kitchen, preparing supper. I expected the aroma of cooking food, the clanking of pots and pans and flatware. But Jo wasn't in the kitchen. And she wasn't in the bedroom, or the study, or in the back yard. Her car was not parked in its usual place in the driveway."

Marvin used his fork to stir the fries on his plate. He had not eaten anything and the food was getting cold.

"I dialed her cell phone," he said, "Her voice mail came on. I was leaving her a message when I saw the note. It was on the kitchen table, plain as the nose on my face."

Marvin retrieved a folded piece of paper from his shirt pocket. He unfolded it. It had been crumpled and uncrumpled. Tears had bled the ink in several places.

"Can I read you the letter, pastor?" he said.

"Yes, Marvin," Pastor Robbins said.

Marvin sipped his iced tea and cleared his throat: *"Dear Marvin, I can no longer live with you. I do not love you as I once did. I have found someone else, someone who has captured my heart. I am leaving to be with him. You do not know him, and it would not matter if you did. You are a kind and gentle man, Marvin, but I need more than you can give me. I need excitement, travel, new faces, new places. My new lover gives me all this and more. Do not try to call me. Do not try to find me. Our marriage is over. Forgive me, and do not hate me for going where my heart is leading. Good-bye, Marvin. With respect, Jo."*

Marvin folded the paper tenderly and placed it in his pocket.

"Can you believe that, pastor?" he said. "Isn't that the most horrible thing you've ever heard?"

"It is bad, Marvin," Pastor Robbins said.

Even now, two weeks after he first held that note in his trembling hands, Marvin's legs would become straw as he thought of it. He would have to sit. He would cry a little and wonder where Jo could be, wonder if her new man was good-looking, wonder how she could have fallen in love with someone else, where he had gone wrong.

"You know what I do almost every hour of every day, pastor? I ask myself this question: What little thing, or big thing, or series of things did I do to wash away from my beautiful Jo the feelings she once had for me? And you know what else? I can never answer that question. I can never answer it."

Marvin removed his glasses and used a napkin to wipe his eyes.

"And sometimes I think I can't take another step," he said. "And I've even wished that the breath in my lungs will be my last breath. Do you know what I'm saying?"

"No Marvin, I don't," Pastor Robbins said. "But the Lord knows."

Marvin looked out the restaurant window. He wanted to see beyond his own reflection, but his eyes would not allow it. He put his glasses on and turned to the pastor.

"There is one bright thing in this whole mess," Marvin said. "I was at the post office a few days ago. I saw this package in my box. It was small, small enough to fit in the box. At first I though it was a letter from Jo, you know, saying she wanted to come back. It was plainly wrapped, with no return address. I laid it on the table in the post office and ripped it open, but it wasn't a letter. It was this."

Marvin took a small carving of Jesus from his briefcase.

"As soon as I saw this," he said. "I just felt a great amount of comfort. Look at the eyes in this little statue, pastor. They sparkle, don't they? Like Jesus is alive in this little piece of wood."

Pastor Robbins held the statue.

"The eyes do seem to have some life in them, Marvin," he said. "It's uncanny."

"I don't know about you, pastor, but this simple little object gives me hope," Marvin said. "It's strange, because I don't know who sent it to me. I was thinking it might be you."

"No, it wasn't me, Marvin," Pastor Robbins said. "But I wish it had been. This is beautiful work."

"Well, whoever it was, it was mighty thoughtful of them," Marvin said. "I'm grateful for it. I think it just might have saved my life."

CHAPTER 2

Ransom Wallace expected trouble from his 35-year-old pickup truck. It didn't surprise him when it backfired, echoing off houses and trees and street signs. Ransom slumped lower in his seat.

The truck crept past Dogwood Auto Parts, made a right onto Main Street and slowed as it passed the old, stately homes facing both sides of the street.

Ransom took mental notes of each house. He studied driveways, fences, the positions of yard lights. He strained his neck in search of signs that there might be dogs at these homes.

He passed Dogwood Community Church and sneered when he remembered the AA meetings he'd attended years ago in the church basement.

He recalled the deacons' decision to discontinue the meetings. They said they'd discovered some of the drunks smoking inside the building on days of bad weather, when they could not smoke outside.

"Don't those people know that when a drunk ain't drinking, cigarettes are sometimes the only things keeping him from drinking?"

Ransom was a little surprised at his own voice as it broke the silence. The hairs on his bare arms stood like soldiers. He rolled up his window against the cool night air.

At the corner of Wilson and Main the old truck lurched as the driver accelerated through the red light. Ransom was pleased at the absence of traffic this time of night. There were few sounds; the far off wail of a freight train struggling against the grade from Hansen Lake; the machine-gunning of a semi truck gearing down at the big curve on the interstate; the slight rumble of his truck on the imperfections in the pavement. He searched for one of the two police cars he knew to be in town, but he did not see either at the intersection.

He turned left onto Sanders Street, and headed north past Johnson's Auto Repair, Ron Marvin's law office and the empty storefront that once housed a branch of an out-of-state bank. He looked to his left at Buddy's Billiards. He laughed as he remembered the fight he got into years ago with a man who refused to pay up on a bet. He thought about just how long ago that was. He shook his head at the quick passage of time, and at his inability to remember the man's name. Between then and now, there had been a marriage gone sour, a four-year prison term, and the accident at the lumber yard that claimed his father's life.

That's just the way things are.

The old truck passed Ralph's 24-Hour Gas and Grocery. Years ago, as an eager teenager with his first public job, Ransom convinced Ralph to stay open all night to accommodate the occasional stray motorist from the interstate. He'd heard Ralph brag about making enough money from these customers to pay his outrageous electric bill and then some. Sometimes, when Ransom tried to list in his mind the good things he'd done in his life, all he could come up with was this one suggestion to Ralph.

Some life.

The lights from the store illuminated the old truck, and Ransom pressed the accelerator. He leaned his head back so the cool blue lights would not shine on his face. Again, he ran a red light, this one at the intersection of Sanders and Wilson. He thought for a moment that he might turn back onto Main Street, for it led directly to the interstate, and the interstate would shorten his travel time. But he did not turn, and instead increased his speed as he passed under the red light. Sanders led back to Main on the west side of town. He took this route and soon he was on the Petersboro Road and out of town.

Darkness enveloped the highway. Ransom checked his rearview mirror and adjusted it to better see the chicken-wire cage in the bed of the truck. The lights of Dogwood, growing dimmer with each turn of his truck's tires, cast a faint glow on the cage, and he saw this light reflected in the eyes of the fruits of his labor: five beautiful breed dogs, alert, scared, panting. Ransom laughed again. He was tired, but content with his take from a town he once called his own.

He turned on the radio and settled himself for the journey, and thought only of the money he would make with those beautiful dogs.

Zilphia Lassiter rose from her bed and checked the clock on the bedside table. She had again over-slept.

"Sleep until you wake up," her doctor told her during her last visit. "This is your body getting the rest it needs. Now that you aren't working, you can sleep as late as your body needs to sleep. This is good for you Zilphy."

All her life she had risen early, always ready to begin her day, always peeking through the window to watch the sun's first burst of color painting the morning sky, always speaking a prayer of thanksgiving to her Father for giving her another morning, another reason to praise him. But in the six weeks since the doctor first diagnosed her terminal cancer, mornings had passed her by. Most days, the sun would already have risen high into the sky before she stepped out of bed. She did not like this, but she had learned to live with it. Pastor Robbins had tried to help her see that God could be found even in her dreary circumstances—and she knew in her heart that this was so—but she struggled to thank him.

"I want more than anything to turn my heart toward Jesus, to praise him for this evil thing that's eating away at my body," she told the pastor during her last visit with him. "But it's difficult, the most difficult thing in the world."

She slipped on her bed shoes and hobbled toward her front door to bring in the morning paper, supporting herself along the way with a chair, a bookcase, the doorknob. She turned the dead bolt and, as its click echoed in the foyer, sensed a strangeness in her soul, a feeling she had not experienced before. She could not immediately identify the feeling, but she knew that if someone had asked her, she would have described it as a sort of holy anticipation.

She opened the door, made sure the morning paper was lying on the front porch, and bent down to pick it up. As she performed this one simple act, the feeling of anticipation swelled. The paper was heavier that usual. She opened it, and gasped when she saw a small wooden plaque tucked between the paper's folds. Because of the strangeness of this object, because her paper was not supposed to contain such a thing, she found herself wanting to fling it into the shrubs beside the porch. But she held onto it and carried the entire bundle into the house and laid it on her kitchen table.

The plaque was about the same length as the folded paper and about half the width. On its face, these words were artfully carved: *"All things work together for good, for those who love the Lord and are called according to his purpose. Romans 8:28."* The words were painted white and were framed by intricately carved vines in several shades of green. The vines hosted tiny flowers of red, yellow, and blue. She was taken by the simple beauty of this thing. She wanted to cry, but resisted. The words on the plaque pierced her heart, a heart that she realized had become hard and spiteful toward her heavenly Father. She sat down, rubbed her fingers across the carved and painted wood, and sobbed deeply. She knew at that moment that Jesus was with her, that he would forgive her coldness toward him, that no matter how damaged she might become by the evil disease devouring her body, Jesus would be there beside her, holding her hand and, if the need arose, he would carry her to be with him in heaven.

She laid the plaque on the table and took bread from the refrigerator. With trembling hands, she placed two slices into the toaster. Even the pushing of the toaster lever had become a chore for her, but this morning the task seemed easier. She buttered the toast and uttered a quiet prayer of thanks for it and for her husband, her sweet Fred, who had made coffee for her before leaving for work.

She ate and stared at the plaque. She wondered who would know that this wonderful thing would be a sort of bandage, binding her broken spirit. She decided that it must have been Pastor Robbins, a young man known in Dogwood for his sluggish preaching, but also appreciated for his many acts of kindness toward others.

CHAPTER 3

Marie Parker eased her foot off the accelerator and turned her small pickup truck onto Gum Swamp Road.

"This is my least favorite part of the route," she said to Nell Calder. "This road's the worst one for twenty miles around. In summer it's like riding on a washboard. In winter, if you don't drive straight down the middle, you're likely to get stuck or spin out into the ditch. In between, it's either dusty or something else."

Nell, sitting in the passenger side of the truck, would be taking over Marie's route in a week.

"When they told me I was going to be postmistress, I screamed a big one," Marie said. "A happy scream, you know, for the promotion and for the fact that I wouldn't have to drive down this road any more."

"What's so bad about it, Marie?" Nell asked. "Besides it being unpaved and all?"

"It's not the driving it that's so bad," Marie said, careful to keep her eyes on the road. "It's the fact that the road's three miles long and there's only two houses on it. The Tarkingtons, they live just up here and they're not so bad. But when you get down to the dead end you're at Raymond Fulcher's house. He's got more dogs than a person should be allowed to have, and well, his place is kinda spooky to me."

"You mean Ray, the hermit?"

"Yeah. The hermit."

Marie pulled the truck over to the Tarkington's box and Nell placed a bundle of mail into it.

"You can tell a lot about a person by the mail they get," Marie said as she eased the truck onto the road. "Take Ray Fulcher. Every month he gets a check from the Veteran's Administration, so I figured he was in some kind of war or something. He also gets a bunch of catalogs, and he subscribes to a few magazines, mostly from religious groups I never heard of—probably cults or something weird like that—and now and then he'll get a letter from a person in Japan, same last name as his. I figure it's his son or maybe a nephew or brother. And he mails that same person a letter each month on the same day, the 10th of the month, like clockwork. Of course, he gets the same junk mail as the rest of the folks—excuse me, Nell, we don't call it junk mail, we call it prepaid, the bread and butter of the U.S. Postal Service."

Both women laughed.

"But Marie, what does he look like? The hermit I mean?"

"I really don't know," Marie said. "I've seen him in town in that old pickup of his, but only from a distance. His house sits way back, probably a couple hundred yards from the road. You can't really see it from the mailbox, because of all the trees. But I've heard it's creepy, with grass growing knee high everywhere, and junk all over the yard and chickens and hogs wandering around the place, and trees with limbs hanging down so low that they touch the roof of the house everywhere. And the dogs, Lord have mercy. In a second you'll see what I'm talking about."

Marie negotiated the bumpy road and Nell took notice of the landscape around them. At the Tarkington place, the land was mostly cleared and hosted well-manicured fields of corn, soy beans and cotton on both sides of the road. The Tarkington's barns were well-kept and their farming equipment sat neatly under shelters. Just beyond the last field, the road dipped suddenly into a ravine and the scenery changed from open fields to thick woods.

The truck rumbled over the bridge at Gum Creek. Nell shivered. All this talk about the hermit had given her an uneasy feeling. As they approached the hermit's mailbox, she could see why Marie did not like to come here. Large trees—gums, oaks, cypress, swamp maples—lined the road on both sides. Large vines—like giant snakes—shot up from the swamp floor and wrapped themselves around the trees.

The truck approached Ray Fulcher's driveway. Dogs poured from the woods like ants to a picnic. There were at least a dozen, some large breeds, a few small ones. They seemed to be well mixed, a sort of canine stew. And they were dirty, though well-fed.

The dogs ran for the truck and barked in unison.

"See what I mean, Nell?" Marie said. "Never seen so many dogs in one place. It's the worst stop on the route. They come from everywhere. Sometimes I think they're going to jump right in my truck and eat me alive. And every day it seems there's more of them. Quick, I'll drive to the box and you just shove the mail in and we'll get the heck out of here."

Marie eased her truck to the mailbox. Nell opened it, took out a single piece of outgoing mail, and shoved Ray Fulcher's prepaid bundle into the box. The dogs kept up their racket but made no attempt to come closer than a couple dozen feet of the truck. Nell closed the mailbox lid and laid down the plastic flag. Marie gave the truck a quick turn into the middle of the road, backed up, paying no attention that she might strike one of the dogs, and gunned the engine. The rear tires tossed gravel into the air like bullets and the small truck shot back toward the main highway.

"That was close," Marie said, as the truck rumbled over the washboard ruts in the road. "You can see why I don't like to come way out here, can't you Nell?"

"I guess it wasn't so bad," Nell said. "Those dogs, they just barked a little, like dogs will do. They didn't come close to the truck. They seemed friendly enough."

"Look, Nell," Marie said. "The hermit and his dogs are bad news. Don't let anything fool you about that. The guy's a nasty old man and his dogs are probably wrapped up with rabies and the mange and fleas and God knows what else. And they multiply like rats down there. So just be careful when you drive down this spooky hill to the hermit's house. That's all you need to know."

Nell glanced at the side mirror. A man at the mailbox waved the dust from his face. A short, dark beard hid most of his chin and cheeks. Khaki shorts and a tee shirt hung loosely on his body, which was quite average in height and build. He stood with a slight stoop. His hair was cut short under a baseball cap pulled low on his forehead. Nell could not see the man's mouth, but she guessed that it did not sport a set of fangs, as some people in Dogwood claimed. He took his mail from the box and reached down and scratched the head of a large German shepherd. He knelt by the mailbox and the rest of the dogs surrounded him, their tails wagging.

"So, he's a hermit, huh?" Nell said.

"You better believe it," Marie said. "A real, live hermit."

CHAPTER 4

Ray Fulcher placed the small canvas shoulder bag and the bow saw on the picnic table under his pecan tree.

He walked up the steps and into the screened porch, unbuckled his waders and carefully stepped out of them. He hung them on the hook in the corner. He opened a large plastic barrel, scooped a generous portion of dry dog food, and poured it into a plastic bucket. A small dog nipped at his feet, playfully growling.

"Cool it, Judas. Wait your turn."

Ray dipped into the barrel again and poured the contents into the bucket. He walked into the back yard. Almost immediately the dogs came. They ran from the woods, from behind the storage barn, from under the old pickup truck. Yelping with joy, the dogs surrounded Ray and followed him to the barn, where he poured the contents of the bucket into three large aluminum bowls. The dogs jumped toward the food, each one taking his own spot around the bowls. There was no fighting, no showing of teeth. The dogs simply ate, though the eating was quite feverish.

Ray bent over and placed his arm around the little dog.

"C'mon Judas," he said. "I'll feed you inside. I don't think the big boys are going to let you into the circle today. You get to go into the big house with Poppa."

Ray laughed and looked into the anxious eyes of the little dog.

"You sure are one ugly critter," he said, laughing harder. He thought that if he let go, the little dog's wagging tail just might lift the poor creature into the air.

On the day he'd found Judas at the county landfill, the scrawny animal was scrounging about in the trash, searching for food, shivering like he would fall apart any minute. He had shampooed the little dog, given him something to eat, and, unlike the other dogs that had exercised squatter's rights at his home, had allowed the little one to live inside the house. For a couple of weeks, Ray called the dog "Mutt" simply because he could not think of a better name for such a helpless creature. Then, one afternoon, as he and the dogs were walking back from the mailbox, "Mutt" planted a solid bite on Ray's left heel. The dog's tiny teeth stung like a wasp, and Ray could not determine the reason for the little dog's sudden turn of affection.

"Now, I know what your name is," Ray told the dog. "It's Judas, for you have betrayed my kindness to you with a bite on my foot!"

Ray forgave the dog his bad behavior and kept him in the house. The little dog had become quite good company and had remained faithful and had not bitten him again.

Ray prepared a simple meal, as was his custom. He made a ham and cheese omelet, toasted a couple of pieces of wheat bread, and peeled and sliced an apple. He poured a glass of sweetened iced tea. As he ate, he fed Judas from the table, a habit practiced by Ray as a form of appreciation for the little dog, who had become quite a loyal companion and to whom Ray could reveal his innermost thoughts.

"What I like about you, Judas," he had said more than once. "Is that you can't talk back."

Ray cleaned up the supper dishes and thought about his plans for the next day.

"We've got to straighten up the place a little, Judas. We've got company coming tomorrow and we have to make sure our guests are comfortable. It's our Sunday to host the group."

Since moving to Dogwood, Ray had agreed to host the worship group once every other month, but only after he had finished the repairs and renovations to his home. When he bought the house and accompanying 20 acres from the Tarkingtons, the place needed a handyman's touch. The well-built house had formerly hosted some of the Tarkington's farm workers, and they had taken fairly good care of it. It needed paint and shingles and a good scrubbing. He rearranged the interior walls to open the things up a little, and added new siding and a screened-in porch in the rear. During the renovations, he had missed his wife, Doris, terribly and had often cried at night for her company. Her suffering from Hodgkins disease had been long and extreme and he was relieved for her, and for himself, when she finally walked over from this life to the next. She was his high school sweetheart, his partner, his best friend. Life was not the same without her. But, through the support of the worship group and as a result of many prayers on his behalf, he had come to accept her death and continue with his life. He liked to think that she was sitting in heaven with Jesus, watching him as he worked on the house. He also believed that he had done the right thing by selling their home in Raleigh and moving to the quiet life he had made for himself at the edge of Gum Swamp.

"Now, Judas," he said, hanging the dish towel on the oven door handle. "Let's clean up this place. It looks like a couple of old fuddy-duddy bachelors live here."

Ray worked on the cleaning until late in the evening. He made sure everyone in the group would have a place to sit. He dusted everything, vacuumed the floors, and cleaned the bathroom better than usual. He always looked forward to worshipping with his Christian friends. He felt a special kinship with them, both practical and spiritual. They were, like himself, people who felt a little cast off from normal society, folks who had experienced tough times in conventional churches, or who had grown weary of the staleness that they believed had become a staple in many congregations. These people simply desired a fresh touch from God and had discovered this blessing among other people with similar beliefs and experiences. Ray enjoyed worshipping in people's homes and he and his friends believed that this type of worship was akin to the kind of worship experienced by the very first Christians in the years immediately following the resurrection of Jesus.

"Judas, I believe you need to go outside."

Ray opened the door on the screened porch and watched Judas scamper to the woods just beyond the barn. The sky was clear and the nearly full moon gave the yard a sort of afterglow, casting shadows of trees and buildings. He could see none of the other dogs, many of whom wandered off during the night to prowl around as dogs are supposed to do. He knew morning would bring most of them back for breakfast. And he knew they might bring new friends with them, or that one or two of the usuals would have left for good, searching for better places or different scenery. Ray would feed and water as many as showed up at his barn. He loved the dogs, and appreciated their presence at his home.

Judas finished his business and hurried back across the yard and Ray let him into the house. Judas followed Ray toward the bedroom, keeping as close to his master's moving feet as he could safely follow. Ray knelt at the bed. Judas crouched beside him, his tiny belly on the floor and his front paws stretched forward and crossed.

"Father, I thank you for another beautiful day," Ray said. "You've blessed me today with your love and with my daily bread and with the very breath that keeps me alive. You are so generous in your blessings, Lord, and I receive them in humility and with a grateful heart. I pray that the folks coming to my house tomorrow will be happy to be here and that you will touch us all with your Spirit. Help us, Father, to experience you beyond anything that we may think we know about you. Help my son, Lord, to come to know you. Please send someone to him who will tell him about Jesus in a way that he can understand it. Bless this house, Lord, and bless the people of this community. And, oh yes, thank you for Judas, Lord. Keep him healthy. Amen."

Ray's knees popped as he stood. He removed his bed shoes and settled on the bed. He pulled the covers over himself and reached up to turn off the bedside lamp. A faint whimper rose from the floor beside the bed.

"All right you mangy mutt," he said. "Come on up here."

Judas jumped onto the bed, took his place in the spot where Doris once slept, and snuggled his tiny body just under the warm backbone of his master.

CHAPTER 5

The half moon was high as Ransom pulled the old pickup off the main highway and onto the unpaved path. A wheel struck a pothole and he cursed as the truck shuttered to pull itself out.

"Who would live in a place like this? I'm gonna make him pay me if my truck is damaged."

Ransom checked the rearview mirror and saw that the sudden jerk had dislodged the cage, moving it too close to the edge of the open tailgate.

He cursed again. He stopped the truck and got out. He scanned the area quickly for headlights, taillights, any sign of other vehicles. He grabbed the cage with both hands. One of the dogs, a full-blooded German shepherd, growled and nipped at his fingers.

"Crazy dog!"

He jerked his fingers from the cage. "When I get you out of here, I'll teach you a lesson or two."

He slapped the cage and the dogs began barking.

"I don't believe this."

Ransom scanned the area for anyone who might hear the dogs or see his truck.

He grunted and pushed the cage to the front of the truck bed. He slammed the tailgate shut, but it did not latch. He found a pieced of wire in the bed and tied the tailgate latch to the truck.

"That ought to keep you mutts for a few more minutes. I'll be so glad to get rid of you."

The dogs continued barking and Ransom jumped back into his seat, put the truck in gear and slowly negotiated the dirt path. He drove past an old tobacco barn and the path turned into thick woods. More than a mile into the woods, he spotted a dim light. He left the path and drove through the trees toward the light. He stopped at an abandoned house that tilted severely on its foundation. A lantern hung from a porch post. The house's tin roof had rusted through in several places. Most of the windows were broken and the front porch leaned in the opposite direction of the house's odd tilt. He parked the truck near the lantern.

"I told you I didn't want them dogs barking on the way down here." The voice came from the darkness just beyond the porch.

Ransom got out of the truck and approached the voice.

"It won't my fault," he said. "If you'd fix that path, my truck wouldn't jerk around so much and if my truck didn't jerk around so much those dogs wouldn't bark."

A pudgy man limped from behind the tree. His cap was pulled down on his forehead. Ransom could not see the man's eyes.

"If I fixed my path, someone just might drive back here and discover something I don't want discovered," the man said. "And if you don't stop being such a smart aleck, you just might discover a fist in your face."

Ransom clamped his lips shut. He didn't want to get into an argument with Donnie Keech. He'd argued with Donnie before and the argument, and the resulting fistfight, had gone Donnie's way. He knew another fight with Donnie might draw a weapon other than fists, for Donnie Keech was known to have badly injured people who crossed him.

"I got five dogs," Ransom said. "Good ones. Breed dogs. They ought to be worth more."

Donnie walked to the back of the truck and shone a flashlight on the dogs. They had stopped barking and were huddled together in a mass of fur and paws and ears and tails.

"Breed dogs don't make no difference to me," Donnie said. "Most of these breed dogs make lousy fighters. They've been pampered, taught to do tricks, most of the meanness drilled right out of 'em. They ain't worth more just because they're high bred."

"But, I took more risks getting these dogs, thinking you'd give me more," Ransom said.

"The risk is yours to take, not mine," Donnie said. "I'll give you a hundred dollars for all of 'em."

"Come on, Donnie, you know that ain't enough. They're full-blooded and in good shape. A hundred won't make it worth my while, especially since I been on the road so long to get here."

"A hundred," Donnie said. "Take it, or get yourself outta here and take your mangy dogs with you."

Donnie shone the flashlight into Ransom's eyes. Ransom turned away and waited a moment for his eyes to re-adjust to the darkness.

"OK. I'll take the hundred."

Donnie stuffed the flashlight in his arm pit, pulled a roll of money from his pocket, and counted out five twenties. Ransom stuffed the money into his pocket and untwisted the wire holding the tailgate shut. The gate flew open with a crash and the dogs started barking. Donnie slammed his flashlight into the cage and the startled dogs hushed. He and the driver jerked the cage and it crashed to the ground behind the truck. The dogs whimpered, their eyes open wide in terror.

"I'll be lucky to get these flea-bitten high-society mutts outta here without someone hearing that God-forsaken barking!" Donnie said. "Next time don't bring me no high-falutin' breed dogs."

"I doubt there'll be a next time, " Ransom said, stepping back into the driver's seat. "You don't pay enough."

"You'll be back," Donnie said. "You ain't never made such easy money in your life."

Ransom knew Donnie was right. Gathering dogs for the fights was easy work. Grab them, put a rope around their necks, jerk them into the pen, bring them to Donnie Keech, get your money, and spend the money. And in Dogwood, where the police are usually no where in sight, the pickings had been easy.

"See ya next time," Donnie said. "Same place, same night of the week."

Donnie slapped his hand on the old truck and the hollow sound echoed through the woods. Ransom rolled up his window so that he would not hear the echo, for it reminded him of the hollow feeling that often echoed inside his own heart. Ransom knew then that he would stop at that little bar just down the highway. He had five twenty-dollar bills in his pocket, and he knew just what to do to make all the hollow feelings disappear.

CHAPTER 6

When he saw the plain cardboard box in his roadside mailbox, Jake Stanley had a feeling that began as a tightening of muscles and skin at the base of his neck and ended like a cinder block dropped into the pit of his stomach.

He knew right away the box contained a bomb.

He tried but he could not recall an enemy that hated him enough to place a bomb in his mailbox. He could not recall any enemies at all.

He reached for the box, but his heart shifted gears and he decided then and there to call the police. He always thought it better to be safe than sorry. Sometime earlier, he had read in the Raleigh paper of a man who had opened his mailbox one day only to have his hand blown off by a pipe bomb. That man was a known drug dealer who had done something to anger one of his partners in crime. And, of course, Jake Stanley was just an auto mechanic, and a good and honest one at that, and a well-liked person and a faithful member of Dogwood Community Church and he had no such enemies. Still, he didn't want to take any chances.

He hurried back to the house, picked up the phone and dialed the Dogwood police.

"Who are you calling?" asked Jake's wife, Sara.

"The police," he said. "Hush now, they're answering."

"The police?" Sara said. Her eyes widened. "Is it Rene? Have you heard from Rene? Oh my God, is she OK?"

"No, it's not Rene," Jake said. "I haven't heard from her. You'd be the first to know if I did."

The police dispatcher answered and Jake told her that his mailbox contained a strange cardboard box. He asked if they could send someone over to take a look at it. The dispatcher said she would send someone immediately. She told Jake to stay away from the mailbox until an officer arrived.

"The police'll be here in a minute," he told Sara, hanging up the phone.

"I thought it was about Rene," Sara said. "I don't care about any strange cardboard box in the mailbox. I want to hear from Rene."

Jake laid his hand gently on Sara's shoulder. In the six months since Rene had left home, Sara had changed from a vibrant middle-aged woman into a sad, listless, worrisome person. He thought often of the day their daughter decided to strike out into the world on her own. She was only eighteen, and had just finished high school. She was a good daughter, he thought, and he and Sara were quite shocked to find her note on the kitchen table. He had read the note many times in the past six months, and had memorized it.

"Mom and Dad, Doug and I are running off together. He wants to try to make something of his music. I love him and feel I must go with him. I know you will not approve of my leaving, and that is why I'm doing it this way. I'll call and let you know where I am and how I'm doing. I love you both very much. Rene."

Jake and Sara had asked the police for help, but the police told them Rene was no longer a minor and could go anywhere she wanted without her parents' permission. Rene had called only once in the six months, about a week after she left. She and Doug were on the road, she'd said, and she did not know where they would stop, or which town they would call home, if any.

Jake and Sara had not heard from her since and did not know where she was living or if she was eating or if she had clothes to wear. Sometimes the thought of all this seemed like a heavy rock on Jake's shoulders. He would often hear Sara crying in the bedroom at all times of day or night. He and Sara had prayed together. They had prayed with Pastor Robbins, with friends and family. They had given their daughter's protection to the Lord, but none of this sufficed. Their hearts were broken and would remain so until they saw Rene again. Pastor Robbins had told them not to worry, that worry showed a lack of faith, and this had only made things worse. Now, because of the young preacher's remarks, Sara refused to attend church.

"Chief Norris will be here in a minute," Jake said. "I'll go out and wait for him by the road."

"Do you suppose the box is from Rene?" Sara asked.

"I doubt it. There is no address on it. Marie didn't deliver it. Someone just placed it in the mailbox. It's barely taped shut. I don't think it's from Rene."

"Maybe it is a bomb," Sara said. "And maybe we should bring it in the house and let it explode. That would certainly help end our misery."

Jake did not respond to his wife's foolish remark. Most of the time, Sara was as normal as could be expected, but now and then she would say something like that. He knew those words came from deep within her broken heart, and that they were not the words of the true Sara, the Sara he loved and cherished so deeply. Yet, the words bothered him more than he allowed Sara to know.

Chief John Norris of the Dogwood Police Department turned his car into the driveway as Jake got to the road. The chief got out of his cruiser and approached Jake cautiously, as was his habit, even with people he had known for many years.

"What's going on Jake? Debra said you called and said something about a bomb in your mailbox."

"Yes, I called," Jake said. "But I don't know if it's a bomb or even what it is. It's just a strange cardboard box. Nothing written on the box, no way to tell what's inside. I remember reading about that guy in Raleigh who got his hand blown off when he opened his mailbox. Maybe I'm just being crazy, but I don't want to take any chances."

"Don't blame you for that, Jake. Let's have a listen."

Chief Norris placed his face as close to the mailbox as he dared.

"It's not ticking, Jake," he said. "And I don't smell anything out of the ordinary."

"Maybe you should call the bomb squad," Jake said.

"We don't have a bomb squad, Jake."

"But the sheriff's got one in Petersboro. You could call them."

"Jake, calling the bomb squad is serious business," Chief Norris said. "That's just something you don't do every day. Besides, I got a better idea."

He walked back to his cruiser and radioed the dispatcher. "Debra, send Rufus out to Jake Stanley's house. Tell him to bring his long float."

"His long what, sir?"

"His long float. Just tell him that. He'll know what I'm talking about."

"Yes sir."

Rufus Baker arrived a few minutes later, followed by a convoy of vehicles, including the chief of the Dogwood Fire Department, Mayor Levi Smith, and Mike Dudley, editor of the Dogwood Gazette. All of them had heard the dispatches on their police scanners.

Chief Norris and Rufus wasted no time. They retrieved Rufus's long concrete float from the truck, added the extension to make it about 14 feet in length and walked together toward Jake's mailbox. Chief Norris had positioned his police cruiser between the mailbox and the crowd. He told everyone to find cover behind a vehicle, and they obeyed, except Mike Dudley, who continued snapping photographs. Chief Norris and Rufus stood behind the chief's car, extended the long concrete float toward

Jake's mailbox, and swung it hard. The float struck the mailbox and knocked it off its post. The mailbox hit the ground just as Chief Norris and Rufus ducked behind the cruiser.

Everyone waited for the explosion that didn't come.

One by one, beginning with Chief Norris, the people emerged from their cover. The mailbox had landed in the ditch by the road. The box inside had tumbled out, and the tape holding it shut had pulled back.

Chief Norris waved his hands as a signal for everyone else to stay back. He walked cautiously to the box. He examined its contents and smiled.

"It's OK guys. It's not a bomb. Just some kind of figurine, like a carving or something. There's no danger."

The men ran to the ditch. Mike Dudley snapped a few photos of the figurine, which had fallen almost all the way out of the box.

"It's a carving of a cross," Mike said. "And there's a girl at the foot of the cross, kneeling and praying. It's beautiful. But it ain't a bomb."

Jake stared at the carving. He picked it up. The others had walked back to their vehicles. Jake stood there with the carving in his trembling hands. A tiny tear welled in his eyes. The girl in the carving, though her face was not showing, bore a

Chatham County Libraries
500 N. 2nd Avenue
Siler City, North Carolina 27344

remarkable likeness to Rene. And for some reason he could not explain, he felt a wave of joy pulse through his heart. Rene is going to be all right. She is going to be just fine.

"I wonder who could have put that in your mailbox, Jake," Mike Dudley said.

Jake did not answer. He held the carving close to his chest and ran toward the house. He could not wait to show it to Sara.

CHAPTER 7

I can't believe you thought that was a real bomb in Jake Stanley's mailbox," Boyd Johnson said, peering over the lip of his coffee cup at his friend John Norris.

"What matters is that Jake thought it was a bomb," Chief Norris said. "Now, quit making fun of me and pass me the cream."

Boyd slid the small wicker basket to his friend. Chief Norris took three packets of creamer from the basket, opened them and stirred the contents into his coffee. He raised his hand at Hazel, who was in the back of the grill replacing a plastic bag in a trash can.

"Be right there, Chief," Hazel yelled. "Having a little trouble with the trash bag."

She stretched the bag over the top of the can, set the can on the floor and walked to the table.

"What'll you have, Chief?" she said. "I got a special on a new biscuit. Made it up just for you. I call it the Sausage Bomb Biscuit."

Hazel and Boyd laughed. So did the folks in the next booth, both of whom Chief Norris had never seen before in Dogwood.

"Very funny," he said. "What's those folks over there going to think of law enforcement in this town if you're making fun of the chief of police?"

"Don't matter," Hazel said. "As long as the people who live here respect and admire you, what does it matter what a stranger thinks. I just hope they don't have a bomb in their coffee cups."

Boyd laughed again, spitting some of his coffee on the newspaper. Chief Norris shot Hazel a look that would cut sheet metal. She hushed and got out her pen and order pad.

"Just a biscuit with some jelly, grape," he said. "And make sure you write it down so you won't forget it between here and the counter. And bring Boyd a bib."

"Very funny, Chief," Hazel said. "Just having a little fun. You don't have to get personal."

"Me? Get personal? Just having a little fun, Hazel."

Hazel huffed and walked to the counter to get Chief Norris's biscuit and jelly.

"What *were* you thinking out there, John?" Boyd said. He dabbed coffee from his chin and laid the napkin on the newspaper.

"I was thinking that a man called me and told me he thought he had a bomb in his mailbox," Chief Norris said. "I'm trained, Boyd, trained not to take anything for granted, to take everything seriously until proven otherwise. I did the right thing."

"Maybe you did, " Boyd said. "But a bull float? Whatever gave you that idea?"

"It worked, didn't it?"

"I guess so," Boyd said. "Reminds me of McGiver, though. You know, the guy on TV who's always getting himself out of trouble by making things out of junk lying around him. You know what I'm talking about."

"Unfortunately I do," Chief Norris said.

"But all it was was a wood carving. That's what I read in the Gazette," Boyd said.

"You read right," Chief Norris said. "It looked like a girl bowing down beneath a cross or something like that. Jake said it looked like Rene, but from what I could see the carving didn't have a face."

"How's that going anyway?" Boyd said.

"How's what going?"

"The Rene thing. Last I heard, Jake and Sara hadn't heard from her in six months."

"As far as I know, she's still gone," Chief Norris said. "I put some information about her on the network, but like I told Jake, she's eighteen and can do whatever she wants. I'm sorry for Jake and Sara, but there's not much law enforcement can do, especially since she left on her own accord."

"Yeah, too bad," Boyd said. "That's why I never had children."

Chief Norris laughed. "You never had children, Boyd, because you never got married. At least not yet."

"Funny," Boyd said. "I'm waiting for the right one to come along. My turn will come some day."

"Sure," John said. "I won't hold my breath."

"You're kinda snippy today, John," Boyd said. "What's up, beside bombs and carvings?"

"Well, I sorta dread going into the office, that's all."

"Don't we all?" Boyd said.

"It's Miss Adams. She called me early this morning. I was out feeding my chickens. She called me on the cell phone, though I don't for the life of me know how she got my cell number.'

"I know how she got it," Boyd said. "She's Nora Adams, and Nora Adams always gets what she wants."

I guess you're right," Chief Norris said. "She said her dog, that pure-bred German shepherd she's got, she said somebody stole it last night. Said she wants to meet me in my office first thing."

Hazel brought Chief Norris's biscuit. She flopped the plate on the table and the biscuit nearly rolled out of the plate.

"Sorry, Chief," Hazel said. "But you know how us dummies are. Can't even hold a plate properly, especially with a heavy old biscuit on it."

Boyd laughed and Chief Norris shook his head.

"Beside, if you ask me, it's all in the way you handle her," Hazel said.

"Handle who?" Chief Norris said.

"Nora Adams."

"You were listening to my conversation with Boyd," Chief Norris said.

"Couldn't help but hear it," Hazel said. "What dumb people lack in brains, they make up in other senses, like hearing."

"You guys are a regular sit-com this morning," Chief Norris said.

"Like I said," Hazel said. "Miss Adams is tough, so you got to be tough right back. How do you think a little old scraggly woman like that has survived in this town all these years? She's had to be tough."

"Nora Adams has survived in this town all these years because she's sitting on a pot full of money," Boyd said. "It's easy to be tough when you're rich."

"I ain't rich and I'm tough," Hazel said.

"Right," Boyd said.

Chief Norris gulped the last swallow of coffee in his cup, laid three dollars on the table and stood to leave.

"Well," he said. "You guys can blabber all day long if you like. I've got hard work to do."

Chief Norris opened the door and the little bell jingled.

"But Chief," Hazel said. "You didn't eat your biscuit."

"Sorry, Hazel," he said. "I debated on which was the most difficult thing on my agenda this morning, Nora Adams or your biscuit. As you can see, I've made my decision."

Boyd laughed and the door jingled again and Chief Norris walked up the street.

"They let anybody be in law enforcement these days," Hazel said.

CHAPTER 8

Chief John Norris plopped his keys on the glass-topped desk next to the photograph of his father. He sat in his swivel chair and it squeaked like a rusty swing. He looked at his dad and at former mayor Ernie Capps, who stood beside Jacob Norris in the photo. Both men, dressed in camouflage, held shotguns in one arm and wild turkeys in the other. He smiled at his father and laughed at Ernie Capps.

He remembered 1985, the year then-mayor Capps stumbled upon what he considered a brilliant idea.

"We need to put Dogwood on the map," Mayor Capps told the 203 people who had gathered at Town Hall.

"We're on the map," one man interrupted. "Right between Petersboro and Fayetteville. In fact, we're the smallest dot on the map, if you can even call it a dot."

The crowd erupted in laughter. Mayor Capps pounded his gavel to restore order.

"I'm serious," the mayor said. "We need an attraction that will bring people to our town to spend money."

The mayor launched into a long tirade about the fact that during the Revolutionary War, British General Cornwallis, in the midst of his Southern Campaign, had camped with his Redcoats just east of Gun Swamp on land that now encompassed the entire town of Dogwood. Most of the folks at the meeting knew the story already and many of them were yawning by the time the mayor had finished.

"What we need to do is capitalize on history," the mayor said. "Everybody's doing it, and why should we be any different. Nostalgia sells, my friends. I have a vision of a monument out by the Petersboro Road, gift shops with Revolutionary War themes, an annual re-enactment, the works. Now, I open the floor to anyone who will share my vision."

No one raised a hand. No one stood to speak. After a few minutes of this display of mass unconcern, Mayor Capps pounded his gavel, waking several folks in the process.

"You people beat all," the mayor said. Then he stomped out of the building.

Of course, the mayor's attitude did not set well with the people of Dogwood and Ernie Capps was soundly defeated a year later by Virginia Gooch, the town's first female mayor, who served two consecutive terms without making a single suggestion regarding the town's improvement. She did, however, convince the Department of Transportation to add Main Street to its list of state-maintained roads. The result was a fresh layer of pavement and new striping. For her efforts, Mayor Gooch was awarded, on her last day in office, a nice plaque of appreciation and a three-day, four night Bahamas cruise.

Chief Norris laughed again and thumbed through a pile of papers on his desk, not paying attention to any one of the papers in particular.

Chief Norris gave the first four missing dog reports to Officer Lonnie Wilbert. The chief was, after all, the top law enforcement officer in Dogwood, and though there were only two officers in town—he and Officer Wilbert—there were just some things that the chief did not need to be bothered with.

Not that there was lots of crime in Dogwood. In his 15 years as chief, John Norris had investigated only two major crimes: the armed robbery of Medlin's Drug Store (by an out-of-towner who came into town off the interstate highway) and the night Joe Bryson, crazed with alcohol, unintentionally set fire to his car with a wayward cigarette, and crashed the car into the front of Jackson's Tires, causing a blaze that took out three of the town's 22 businesses. Today there had been the false bomb scare at Jake and Sara Stanley's and now Miss Nora Adams, whose dog was among those missing, had insisted on speaking with "the chief himself" and was sitting across the desk from him.

Sometimes Chief Norris found great humor in the person of Nora Adams. She was quite wealthy, the richest person in Dogwood, yet she carried herself with the air of a common woman. She was thin and wiry, probably in her late seventies, and her attire consisted mostly of smock-type pastel-colored dresses. She drove around town in a 1965 Chevrolet that she claimed she bought new in the fall of 1964. The chief had no reason to doubt this claim, for the old Chevy was the only car he could remember seeing her driving, even when he was a young boy. Miss Adams lived in the largest house in town, an imposing plantation style home with large columns, several balconies, a slate roof, and a wrought iron fence that surrounded the well-kept yard like a sentinel. She gave lots of money to Dogwood Community Church, as evidenced by the number of times her family name appeared on such things as hymnbooks, offering plates, stained glass windows, pews, Sunday school classrooms, and, most recently, the new wheelchair lift.

And now, this tiny but powerful woman was staring down Chief John Norris.

"This isn't like Sparks to be gone for so long," Miss Adams said, dabbing her wrinkled eyes with a well-used tissue. "I let him out into the yard four times a day to, you know, do his business, and to run around a little. Sometimes he runs out the gate in the back, which I keep ajar for that purpose, and down to the field behind the school, but always stays in my sight. When I call, he always comes back in. But today, well, he just vanished."

Chief Norris felt badly for her. He knew how much she loved her German shepherd, Sparks. The dog was a great comfort for the old lady, who had never married and who lived a mostly solitary life.

"I'm sorry about Sparks," Chief Norris said. "Officer Wilbert has taken four other reports of missing dogs today. Bob Jones's rottweiler, Mamie Wilson's collie, Mr. Tucker's bulldog, and Sammy Bender's golden Labrador retriever. Officer Wilbert has checked at the county dog pound and none of them are there. I'm thinking maybe these dogs, and your dog too, got out of their yards and somehow got together and are just roaming around in a pack somewhere. I have a feeling they'll all come home pretty soon."

Miss Adams blew her nose into the tissue. Chief Norris thought the diamond ring on her finger might weigh more than she did.

"I don't think so," she said. "My Sparks is gone for good. I just know it. That dog was such a blessing to me, and now someone has taken him away. I don't know what I'll do if my Sparks is dead, or if he's been stolen and sold to somebody else in a town far away. He was a pure bred shepherd, with papers, you know, and very valuable. But he was worth more than money to me. And besides, my dog would never just take up with a pack of mongrels as you have suggested. I resent that idea to the very core of my being."

"I'm sure he wouldn't do that, Miss Adams," Chief Norris said. "Officer Wilbert and I are going to do all we can to find Sparks and the other dogs. I promise."

"Please try hard," Miss Adams said. "Sparks is all I've got. It's just me and him in that big house. He keeps me company, makes me feel safe. I need him to come home."

Miss Adams rose slowly from her chair and then sat slowly down again.

"Young man, I remember when your father was chief of police in this town."

The old lady raised her hand and pointed a bony finger at the chief.

"He was a good police officer, and he kept things in order around here."

"Yes ma'am, he was, and he did, and I thank you."

"And I was hoping that when you took over his job, God rest his soul, that you would be as good as he was. There was never any crime in our fine town while he was in this office. And, well, I'm not so sure that we're as safe in Dogwood since your daddy passed on. I mean, well, you just think about it."

Nora Adams rose from the chair again, grabbed the cane that she had hooked onto the chair's arm, and hobbled toward the door.

"And there's one other thing that you shouldn't forget, young man," she said, turning to face Chief Norris. "I pay taxes in this town, lots of them, taxes that are spent for lots of things, including the salary of the chief of police."

"Yes ma'am," Chief Norris said as the old woman waddled through the door. "We'll do the best we can. If Sparks is in our jurisdiction, we'll surely find him."

"Make sure you do that very thing," Miss Adams said. "I expect no less than success from you. And I know you'll not scar the memory of your fine father."

The old lady poked her nose into the air and made her way to the front door. She got into her old car with no trouble, revved the engine, and popped it into gear. She backed into the street and Matt Walker slammed on brakes to avoid hitting the Chevy with his pickup.

"I really do need to find that dog," Chief Norris said. "And soon."

CHAPTER 9

Rain slapped Zilphia Lassiter's windshield and she thought of the time long ago when she and her sister, Ruth, had engaged each other in the mother of all mud fights. They were young girls then, maybe ten and twelve, and the mud was cool and slimy and thoroughly dirty. She tried to remember who had started the skirmish, but that little piece of the past could not find its way out of its secret place in her mind. She smiled at the remembrance and wondered what folks would think of her if she were to challenge Ruth once again with mud. Two old women slinging muck at each other in the front yard. She laughed and switched the windshield wipers to high speed.

"It would rain on the very day I chose to drive to Petersboro," she said. "Lord, you have a strange sense of humor."

She'd called Ruth the night before and they had arranged a lunch meeting at the Dupree House in Petersboro. Ruth lived in Raleigh, and Petersboro was a good halfway point. There were plenty of decent places to eat in Raleigh, but Ruth had insisted that Zilphia not drive that far.

"I'm not dead yet," Zilphia had told her older sister. "I can still drive as good as you."

"I know you can," Ruth said. "And I know that you are invincible, Zilphia Jane Lassiter. But I want to get out of the city. The Dupree House is a cozy little place."

"You think it's nice because of that man, that Claude what's-his-name."

"Bowman, Claude Bowman. But that's not why I like going there. It smells so nice, and the food's pretty good. Those little finger sandwiches are tasty."

"It's not the food and the smell," Zilphia said. "It's Claude Bowman."

"Now, Zilphia," Ruth said. "Claude Bowman is half my age."

"My point exactly."

The rain increased and Zilphia tightened her grip on the steering wheel. She slowed the car a little and leaned forward and squinted, as though leaning toward the rain would allow her to see more clearly through it. Her doctor had told her to drive only when she had to, to pick up things at the store or run short errands in town, but she thought his advice too strict. She'd made up her mind to take at least one long trip each week. She turned on her headlights.

The Petersboro Road, officially known as U.S. Highway 301, had once been part of the most-traveled route from the crowded cities of the north to the constant sunshine of Florida. In its heyday, it was considered a marvel of highway engineering, providing continuous blacktop for hundreds of miles and spewing Florida snowbirds with lots of money to spend into the multitude of small towns along the way. But, since the completion of Interstate 95 some 30 years ago, local Department of Transportation crews had allowed the narrow two-lane highway to fall into disrepair. Part of the slipshod maintenance included a seemingly purposeful neglect of the pavement on the road's shoulders, many miles of which were cracking and falling apart. In a pelting rainstorm, a driver was more likely than not to slide too close to the deteriorating shoulders, resulting in much business for the local realignment mechanics. To avoid this costly hindrance, Zilphia slowed her car to a crawl.

About a hundred yards ahead, a pair of flashing emergency lights were barely visible through the rain, which was now falling in sheets. Zilphia believed she had seen the truck before, though she was not certain if she knew the owner. Her car crept past the truck and she saw that its left front tire was flat. The rain had turned the ground beneath the truck into a chocolate-like mess. A man struggled with a jack that kept sliding on the muddy ground.

"Poor fellow," Zilphia said.

She drove a few feet farther and eased her car onto the shoulder. She looked about for an umbrella, which she already knew was not there. She opened the door and stepped into the deluge. The rain soon soaked her to the skin. But Zilphia was not one for primping and did not mind that she was wet to the bone.

"Ray? Ray Fulcher? Is that you?" She raised her voice above the drumming of the rain on the pavement. But the man with the jack did not hear her. Zilphia walked steadily toward the truck until she was standing beside the man.

"Ray Fulcher. You've gotten yourself into quite a mess," she said.

Ray looked up at her and the rain pelted his face. He stood.

"Zilphia Lassiter," he said. "What in the world are you doing here?"

"Stopping to help a fellow human being," she said, laughing.

"But it's raining cats and dogs, and, you shouldn't be out on a day like this."

"I got a right to be here just as much as you do, Ray Fulcher."

"But…"

"But, like I told Ruth, I ain't dead yet," she said.

Zilphia had been one of the first people Ray had encountered after moving to Dogwood in the spring of 1998. She'd backed her car into his truck in the parking lot at Ralph's Gas and Grocery. The damage to the old truck's bumper was hardly noticeable, but Zilphia had apologized profusely and had offered to reimburse Ray for any expenses incurred in the repairs. Ray refused her money, but because of her unrelenting insistence, he agreed to have lunch with her at Hazel's Grill. Since that incident, he'd seen Zilphia only on his occasional visits to town, but he considered her a friend.

"You still haven't fixed that bumper," Zilphia said, pointing to the dent that had over the years become encrusted with a sheen of rust. "I wish you'd let me pay for it."

"Zilphia," Ray said. "Forget about the bumper. It's not worth fixing. You should get back in your car. You look like…"

"I look like what? A wet dog? Is that what you were going to say?"

"Well, no. You look like you shouldn't be out here getting soaked."

"I stopped to help you, Ray Fulcher." She bent her frail body to get a better look at the jack. "And that's what I intend to do."

"But it's just a flat."

"I can see that," she said. "Now, what do you need me to do?"

Ray stared at Zilphia and held back a laugh. She did look like a wet dog. In fact, she bore a weird resemblance to Judas.

"What're you looking at?" she said. "Let's get that tire changed."

"Anything you say, ma'am," Ray said. "If I could get the jack stabilized, I'd have the job half finished."

"Hang on," Zilphia said. "I'll be right back."

Zilphia walked to her car, retrieved the keys from the ignition, and pushed a button on the key ring. The trunk of her car popped open. She fiddled inside the trunk and lifted a round object. She placed the object on the ground and closed the trunk. She waved for Ray to join her at the car.

"Here," she said. "This ought to keep the jack stable long enough to do what you need to do."

"What is it?"

"It's the top to my old bird bath. I backed over it with my car the other day and cracked the stand to smithereens. I was going to take the top to Miller's in Petersboro, to see if he could match it with a stand. It should work with the jack."

"But the weight of the truck might crack it."

"That would be fine," Zilphia said. "Then I'd have good reason to buy a whole new bird bath."

"If you say so," Ray said. He picked up the concrete top and wondered how a woman as frail as Zilphia could have lifted it. He placed the top beneath the truck's bumper, set the jack on it, and used the tire tool to crank the jack. The jack stayed in place and the truck was soon high enough from the ground to remove the flat.

Zilphia walked around the truck, careful to watch her step on the slick shoulder. She peeked into the cab and was surprised at the cleanliness of it. On the seat lay a newspaper and a pair of gardening gloves. A gun rack hung above the rear window. It held two fly-fishing rods. On the window, a decal allowing the truck to enter the county landfill was peeling from too much exposure to the sun. In the bed, two large bags of dog food lay exposed to the rain.

"I hope your dogs like gravy with their food," Zilphia said. But Ray did not seem to hear her.

As suddenly as it had begun, the rain slacked, then dwindled to a drizzle. Zilphia walked to the rear of the truck and lifted the lid on the huge metal tool box strapped with bungee cords to the flimsy tailgate. There were all sorts of tools; a large hammer, an electric drill, a set of jumper cables, several pipe wrenches. A wooden box, about the size of a cigar box, begged Zilphia to open it. She glanced toward the front of the truck. Ray was using the lug wrench to put the final torque on the lug nuts. She opened the wooden box. Inside were six beautiful chisels, with hardwood handles, brass ferules, and blades of bluish steel. There was a honing stone and a short length of leather, perhaps from an old belt. She ran her finger along the front edge of one of the chisels and jerked it away. She was surprised at its razor sharp feel. The tool left a tiny shallow cut on the tip of her finger.

She picked up the chisel. It felt good in her hand; strong, heavy.

"Well, that just about does it," Ray said. "Zilphia? Where'd you get to?"

Zilphia let go of the lid of the metal tool box and it slammed shut. She stuffed the chisel in her sock and winced as its razor edge nicked the skin just above her ankle. She bent her small body toward the muffler and pretended to be quite interested in the underside of Ray's truck.

"Zilphia?"

"Back here, Ray," she said. "Just looking at your undercarriage. There's a bit of rust under here. You might want to get it checked out."

"My undercarriage? Of course it's rusty, Zilphia. This truck's forty years old. Anything that age is going to have some rust. I had rust when I was forty."

Zilphia laughed and stood and placed her hands on her hips.

"I guess you changed the tire without me," she said. "Sorry I didn't help more."

"But you helped a great deal," Ray said. "Your bird bath top was just what I needed to get that old jack stabilized. I am sorry to say that it cracked, just like I thought it would."

"That's OK," Zilphia said.

"Let me pay you for it," Ray said, reaching for his wallet.

"No, absolutely not," she said.

"But I insist."

"I insist not," she said. She held up her hands and stepped onto the pavement. The sun had peeked from behind the gray clouds and the blacktop was warming. A thin fog rose from the asphalt.

"I can't take money for an act of mercy. It wouldn't be Christian. Let's just say we're even. I dented your old bumper; you cracked my old bird bath. That sounds about even, don't you think?"

"I, well, I guess so," Ray said.

"Done deal then," Zilphia said. "Now, I must meet my sister, Ruth, in Petersboro. We have a lunch date."

"But you're soaked to the bone, Zilphia."

"I'll be dry enough by the time I get to the Dupree House," she said. "Besides, me being so wet and frazzled will give those snooty folks at the tea room something to talk about for weeks. Don't you think?"

"Most certainly," Ray said, laughing.

Zilphia walked to her car and Ray lifted the lid to the metal tool box. He set the lug wrench inside and instinctively replaced the top to the wooden chisel box.

"Wait a minute," he said. "Someone's been…"

He looked toward Zilphia's car, which was already at least a quarter mile away, slicing through the thin fog.

"Nosy woman," he said.

CHAPTER 10

Ruth moved a fork from the right side of her plate to the left. She placed the spoon at the top of the plate, slid the tea cup about four inches to the right, removed the cloth napkin from the cup, and laid it on her lap. She rubbed her hand across the napkin to remove all the wrinkles.

"I can't believe you allowed yourself to get soaking wet," Ruth said. "You look like something the cat dragged in."

"I know," Zilphia said. "But the poor fellow needed help. Turns out I came along just in time. The top to my birdbath did the job nicely."

"They have a bathroom here, Zilphia. Maybe you could go in there and at least find some paper towels to, well, I don't know if there's anything you can do now."

Zilphia laughed.

"I'll be just fine, Ruth," she said. "Stop being such a mother hen."

"Sometimes you need a mother hen," Ruth said.

"Not as much as you need to *be* a mother hen."

Ruth raised her hand. Claude Bowman hurried from the counter, pen and pad in hand.

"I think I'll have the salmon sandwich plate," Ruth said. "And coffee."

Claude scribbled on the pad and turned to Zilphia.

"Just coffee for me," she said. "I'm not too hungry."

"But you have to eat something," Ruth said. "You look like you're famished."

"This look comes with the territory," Zilphia said. "It's the way a soaking wet sick woman is supposed to look. All I want is a little coffee."

"Just coffee," Claude said. He scribbled on the pad, turned, and quickly disappeared through a door to the kitchen.

"He is kinda cute," Zilphia said. "But much too young for you, sister. Maybe young enough to be your grandson."

"Hush that talk," Ruth said. "I'm not interested in Claude Bowman. I'm not interested in any man."

"You've always been interested in any man," Zilphia said.

Both women laughed.

"So, what's going on in Dogwood?" Ruth said. "What's it been? Two weeks, three?"

"Three," Zilphia said. "Same old stuff. Except we've got someone stealing dogs. They got Nora's German shepherd. She all up in the air about it."

"She's always up in the air about something," Ruth said. "What about you, Zilphia? How are you holding out?"

"I have good days and bad," Zilphia said. "The last couple of weeks have been good. I've gotten a lot done. Made sure my will was up to date. Made a list of who gets what in the house. Of course, Fred thinks that kind of thing is morbid. He gets upset."

"I can understand that," Ruth said. She used her napkin to dab her eyes and then returned the napkin to her lap and rubbed out the wrinkles.

"I guess so," Zilphia said.

Claude brought out Ruth's sandwich plate. He poured coffee for both women and walked back to the counter. The sisters did not speak for a long while. Ruth finished her sandwich and dabbed her mouth with the napkin. She folded the napkin and placed it on her plate. She laid the flatware on the napkin and gathered the empty creamer containers and placed them next to the napkin. Claude noticed Ruth's attempt to bus the table. He hurried over, picked up the women's plates, and placed the check on the table.

"Thank you, Claude," Ruth said.

"Yes ma'am."

Ruth looked at the check and then laid it back on the table.

"I just worry about you, Zilphia," she said. "I've been praying that the Lord will heal you, that you'll receive a miracle."

"It'll be a miracle either way," Zilphia said. "If I live or if I die."

"Don't talk about dying, Zilphia. I don't want to hear that."

"We all die, Ruth. When it's our time, the Lord takes us."

"I know. But I still don't like to think about it."

"I'll be OK," Zilphia said. "And so will you. I worried about it for a long time, then the Lord gave me peace. He's with me. He's with you."

Ruth sniffed. She leaned over and hugged her sister. Zilphia did not like hugging, be she accepted her sister's show of affection.

"Let's get out of here," Zilphia said. "The blubbering's getting to me. Next thing you know, Claude Bowman will be over here blubbering too. He looks like he'd be the kind to blubber."

Zilphia picked up the check.

"I'll get that," Ruth said.

"No, let me do it. You may not have me around too much longer to pay your check for you."

Zilphia laughed. She opened her pocketbook and fiddled around for her wallet. She took money out of the wallet and laid it on the table with the check.

"Thanks for the lunch," Ruth said. "I feel better."

"Yeah," Zilphia said. "Nothing like a hardy salmon sandwich to cheer a person up."

Ruth laughed.

"But there is one more thing I need to ask you," Ruth said.

"What's that, sister?"

"Did you know you have a chisel in your pocketbook?"

"Yes, I'm aware of that," Zilphia said.

"But, why—?"

"It's a long story."

CHAPTER 11

Lemuel Banks puffed hard as he lifted the box onto the counter at the Dogwood Post Office.

"Whatever's in there is heavy, Mr. Banks," said Postmistress Marie Parker. "It's gonna cost you a pretty penny to mail it."

"I'm telling you Marie, it's just books, like I said."

"I got to check it anyway, Mr. Banks. Anything that goes media rate has to be checked. All this business of buying and selling on the internet. People are taking advantage and shipping all kinds of stuff media rate."

"Do you have to cut the tape? It took me half an hour just to tape it."

"I sure do."

Marie retrieved a small box cutter from the drawer in the counter. She carefully sliced the tape on the top and sides of the box lid and then opened the box. She removed a layer of folded newspapers and then a stiff piece of half-inch plastic foam, revealing the books beneath.

"See, I told you it was just books. I'm sending them to my brother in Florida. We got this book trading thing going. I send him some, he sends me some."

"OK, Mr. Banks. But I'm just doing my job here."

"Now I got to tape the box back."

"Don't worry about that. I'll re-tape it."

Marie weighed the box, took Lemuel's money, pulled a sticker from the machine and stuck it on the box and gave Lemuel his receipt.

"Next time, if you'll bring the box already opened, I can check it easier and then tape it for you. It'll save a couple of minutes."

"I guess I'll have to do it your way," Lemuel said. "If it ain't one thing it's another. Seems like every day Big Brother's watching us more and more. Why can't things be like they used to be?"

"That's a good question, Mr. Banks."

Marie Parker considered herself blessed to have a job at the Dogwood Post Office. She liked people, or most people, and she enjoyed the hours. The pay and benefits were as good or better than most jobs in town. And now that she had been promoted to postmistress, the pay would be even better and she wouldn't have to drive a route every day. She'd always felt that the Postal Service's motto of "rain, sleet or shine" was a bit much, especially in winter, and she was glad to pass her route along to Nell.

At the post office Marie kept up with most of Dogwood's goings and comings without leaving the office. She considered this a fringe benefit, a sort of re-imbursement for the time spent dealing with so many people. Most of the town's residents came to the post office at least once a week, many of them every day. She enjoyed the latest news without even having to read The Dogwood Gazette. Most days she figured she was quite well informed, and was perhaps the most informed person in town.

This agreeable situation played well on this particular day, for Marie had already begun to formulate a theory as to the disposition of all the missing dogs in town. Miss Nora Adams had come to the post office earlier on her way home from Chief Norris's office, and she had told Marie all about her poor Sparks. Marie had been told also of the disappearances of Bob Jones's rottweiler, Mamie Wilson's collie, and Mr. Tucker's bulldog.

She'd also heard that Sammy Bender's prize golden Lab, Boo, had been taken from Sammy's pickup truck right there in the post office parking lot. Sammy had come into the post office to check his mail. When he returned to his truck, Boo was no where in sight. This was most unusual, Sammy had told Marie, since Boo was a champion Lab and always did exactly as Sammy told him. So far, Miss Adams had been the only dog owner in town to offer a reward for the return of her pet.

"But I'm considering it," Sammy told Marie.

These things were on Marie's mind when Chief Norris walked into the back door of the post office.

"Hi there, Chief," Marie said, turning the key in the cash drawer into locking position. "Sit back there at my desk and I'll be with you in a minute."

Marie removed the cash drawer key and stuffed it in her pocket. She turned off the computer and grabbed a small wad of papers from the front counter. She made her way through mail pouches, boxes and other post office paraphernalia to the back of the building and sat down at her desk. Chief Norris seemed comfortable enough in the small metal chair beside the desk.

"What can I do for you, Marie?" Chief Norris said. "You sounded pretty serious on the phone."

"I am serious, Chief," Marie said. "I'm serious as a person can be."

"Well, tell me what's going on."

"What's going on is that I think I know where all the missing dogs are. I think I've solved the crime for you."

"Wait a minute," Chief Norris said. "How did you know about the missing.... Oh yeah, you work at the post office."

Chief Norris had always been a little envious of Marie's employment at such a strategic position in town. She knew more than he did about most newsy things, and she often knew it hours before anyone came into his office to give an official report. He also knew Marie well enough to remember that once a person is cornered by this talkative young woman, the best strategy is to let her have her say.

"So, tell me your theory."

"Well, it's pretty simple really," she said. "I think the hermit out on Gum Swamp Road is stealing them, the dogs I mean. I think he's sneaking into town, luring them into his old truck with meat or something, and then taking them out to his place. I think you need to go out there and check it out, arrest him, bring those dogs back to the good people of Dogwood."

"The hermit? You mean Ray Fulcher? Stealing dogs? C'mon Marie, you've got to be kidding. Ray

Fulcher wouldn't steal anything. He wouldn't hurt a fly."

"That's what you think, Chief, but let me ask you something. When's the last time you drove out to the hermit's house?"

"Well, it's probably been a few months, maybe a year. I don't know. Maybe two years. I don't ever have a reason to go down there, Marie. My jurisdiction ends just down there at Gum Creek...Yes, that's it. I was down at the creek last summer with my grandson. We went fishing at the bridge. But we didn't go as far as Ray's house, not that far down the road."

"That's what I thought," Marie said. "But, you see, I go out there every day, on my route. Of course, Nell's been training on the route the last couple of weeks, but before that I was there every day. And the hermit's got dogs, Chief, plenty of dogs. And in my opinion, there's more dogs every day. It seems to me that I may have even seen a big golden lab like Sammy Bender's down there, and maybe even a pure bred German shepherd like Sparks. It just makes sense to me that the hermit is taking these dogs. It's the only thing that's logical, because who else would steal dogs like that?"

"But, Marie, Ray's dogs are all strays. I've seen his dogs. They're the mangiest looking bunch of animals in the county. He feeds them, I suppose, but he don't ever wash them or take them to the vet or anything. They spend their days sniffing around the swamp, but I've never heard about any of them hurting anyone or doing any damage. They stick pretty close to Ray, who's not such a bad guy. Why would he want to come into town and steal all those beautiful, pure-bred dogs? Seems to me he'd think he had enough dogs already."

"I'm telling you, Chief, the hermit is the one stealing the dogs. All you need to do is go out there and see for yourself. It's not right, the way he lives all cooped up out there in the swamp. That kind of life is bound to drive someone nuts, if they aren't nuts already. And that kind of nutty person is the kind that would steal anything, even dogs. In fact, if you wait a few hours, you'll probably get a call from Miss Adams telling you that the hermit's brought her Sparks back for the reward money."

"Look, Marie," Chief Norris said. "I can't just go out there and accuse Ray of something he probably hasn't done. I need evidence, a good reason, a reasonable reason for searching someone's property. Just because you think Ray Fulcher is stealing dogs, don't make it so."

"But what about all the people he's had out at his house? That seems kind of suspicious to me," Marie said.

"What people, Marie? Have you been spying on Ray?"

"Well, I wouldn't call it spying. It's just that I went out there one Sunday morning to, er, deliver some, some, er, pre-paid bulk that I'd forgotten to take the day before. And, well, there were probably six or eight cars out there. I couldn't see them really well through the trees—you know how blocked out the hermit's house is—but I'm sure it was something no good. I mean, folks are supposed to be in church on Sunday morning. At least decent folks. There's definitely something going on down there."

"You take the cake, Marie Parker."

"But, Chief…."

Chief Norris stood up and walked toward the back door. He hesitated and turned to Marie. "Look, I'll think about it. And I do appreciate your concern, and your theory. It's a lead of sorts, and I'll try to check it out."

"Thanks, Chief ," Marie said. "Just trying to be a good citizen."

"That you are, Marie. No doubt about it."

Chief Norris walked the half block from the post office to the police station. He glanced around the small downtown area, as was his habit. Old Bobby Wells was sweeping the sidewalk in front of his barber shop. He stopped sweeping and threw his hand up when he saw the chief.

Chief Norris's father first took him to Bobby's barber shop when he was about five years old.

"But I want momma to cut my hair, like always" the young John Norris had argued as his dad plopped him in to the big barber chair.

"It's time for you to get your hair cut like everybody else, like a big boy should," his father said.

"But, I can't."

"Yes you can," Jacob Norris said, looking sternly at his son, holding the wiggly boy in the chair. "And stay still, boy. Bobby can't cut your hair if you're wiggling like a snake. He just might cut your ear off."

Little John Norris screamed at the thought of losing an ear. Jacob Norris looked at Bobby Wells and said, "I guess that was the wrong thing to say."

"No doubt," Bobby said.

Jacob Norris pushed a little on his son's shoulders. "I've got an idea, boy," he said. "Just find something in the room here, something nice to look at, something you like, and just keep your eyes glued on it, and before you know it, the haircut will be over, and you'll be the handsomest boy in town."

Young John Norris turned his eyes to the thing that caught his attention first: his father's police revolver. He stopped yelling. He stared at the pistol, mesmerized by the shiny pearl handle, its sleek blue steel, the warmth of the leather holster. He decided then that he wanted to be a police officer like his dad. And that desire had never left him.

Now, Miss Adams's comments made him think he might not be measuring up to his father's unvarnished reputation. Miss Adams had her doubts. He wondered if others in Dogwood felt the same.

His eyes moved from Bobby Wells to Marty Hamm's hardware store. He was surprised to see Ray Fulcher's old pickup truck at Marty's store. Surprise gave birth to concern when he saw a bunch of dogs in the bed of the truck. One of the dogs was a German shepherd. And one of them bore a striking resemblance to Boo, Sammy Bender's prize-winning golden Lab.

CHAPTER 12

Sometimes Pastor Joseph Conrad Robbins saw himself as a man hanging by a frayed rope over the face of a huge granite cliff, chipping at the massive rock with a tiny pick, knocking off miniscule pieces of granite, the chips falling into a deep abyss below him.

But he kept these thoughts to himself and prayed often that they would be wiped out of his mind forever.

Pastor Robbins dragged a U-Haul into Dogwood in the summer of 1995. He was fresh out of seminary, newly ordained, and ready to change the world for Jesus. With his wife, Karen, and two young sons in tow, he moved into the parsonage of the Dogwood Baptist Church with one strong goal: to bring the entire town of Dogwood—population: 1,424—into the fold of his church—membership: 147.

"This is an all-time low figure for us," the chairman of the pastor search committee had told Pastor Robbins. "We've sort of seen a downward surge in attendance since the beginning of the big fight."

"Big fight?"

"Yeah. Nothing to be alarmed about, though. Even the most beautiful garden's got to be weeded out now and then."

Joseph Robbins assured the members of the search committee that he was the man to bring the numbers up again, that he was the one who would redeem Dogwood Baptist Church and return this mighty body of believers to its former glory as the dominant spiritual power in town. And, though Pastor Robbins's preaching lacked power, the search committee—and ultimately the fledgling congregation—felt that a young man with a young family would be just the thing to energize the church.

But today, sitting in his leather-covered chair in the pastor's study, Joseph Robbins could think only of his failures as a minister. He thought of the heated discussions his congregation had engaged in shortly after his arrival; how one half of the membership had argued vehemently for what they called "old-fashioned doctrine," while the other half had politicked heavily in favor of a "more tolerant view" of things; how ultimately this fight resulted in the loss of more members and the eventual vote to exit the denomination altogether; how this 150-year-old church had pulled itself out of the ashes of a holy war with a new name and a new focus: Dogwood Community Church, non-denominational.

Through it all, Pastor Robbins remained. In his heart, he knew the Lord had brought him to this tumultuous congregation. More importantly, the members had always paid him well and given him a nice home in which to live, and he could not afford to move away, to start over in another place, to take his boys out of school, to go to all the trouble of working with another pastor search committee, to do any of that. He harbored in his heart the glorious memories of seminary, and the call of God on his life, and a faint recollection of what it meant to be on fire for Jesus.

Pastor Robbins closed his book of sermon illustrations. He got up from his chair, walked to the closet, opened the door and picked up a guitar case. He laid the case on his desk and popped open the clasps. The scent of old rosewood brought back memories of happier times, when this same guitar had been a comfort to him and a light for others. He found a hand towel in the case and carefully cleaned the dust from the beautiful instrument. The guitar had been a gift from his father on his sixteenth birthday. And the Lord had used the instrument many times to bring blessing and comfort to people. He rolled the pad of his index finger over the strings. He was surprised that even after a long sojourn cooped up in a closet, the strings had kept their tuning. A light glazing of rust coated the bronzes, but the notes rang true.

He placed the guitar strap around his shoulder, walked down the hall and into the pulpit. He switched on the PA system and strummed the guitar again. He was pleased with the amplified sound. He strummed again, and he sang.

"Keep me simple, Lord.
Keep my eyes on you.
Teach me how to hear your voice.
Show me how to wait on you.
Let me see that you are here.
Keep me simple, Lord."

His voice wavered, tears filled his eyes. But he did not stop singing.

"Keep me like a child,
Always trusting you.
Let me feel your arms around me
In the night when I'm afraid,
When it seems I've lost my way
Keep me like a child.
Keep me simple, Lord.
Keep me simple, Lord."

His fingers, shaking, barely formed the chords on the strings. But he held them and strummed and cried into the microphone. The tears felt good to him and seemed to wash something in him, to bring cleansing, and a certain kind of power, and another flood of memories. He strummed the last chord once more and stood in silence and listened until the hum of the strings faded to nothing.

"That was very nice, preacher."

Pastor Robbins turned quickly into the direction of the voice. Zilphia Lassiter leaned on the piano by the side door. Her frail body reminded him, as it always did, of a withered plant. He remembered then that it was 2 p.m. on a Friday. Zilphia Lassiter always visited him at that time.

"I didn't know you played the guitar," she said, slowly making her way toward the pulpit, holding on to the end of each pew, stepping gingerly, as if walking on ice. "Your song was beautiful. And you did it so well, in spite of the crying."

"I didn't mean for anyone to hear it," Pastor Robbins said. "It was just, I mean, I hadn't taken my guitar out in years and well…."

"And the song. I don't think I've heard it before. Where did you get it? It was beautiful."

"Oh, it's just a song I composed years ago, while I was in college, before seminary. I used to sing it quite often, but now, well, I haven't sung it in years."

"You wrote that song? Preacher, you've been hiding your light under a bushel. You ought to sing it in church sometime. I'd bet a lot of people would love to hear it. And they'd love to hear you play your guitar. It was very moving for me."

"I probably won't do that," he said. "I'm sort of rusty, like these strings. And, well, I just like to play for myself these days, myself and the Lord, when I play, that is."

"You should let your light shine before men, preacher. And, Lord knows, this church could use some light."

Zilphia laughed, but Pastor Robbins didn't. He leaned his guitar on the podium, found a tissue beside the pulpit Bible, and wiped his eyes with it.

"I think it's sweet when men cry," Zilphia said. "Especially when they're crying about the Lord, or what the Lord's done for them. Too many men think they aren't supposed to cry, that it's a sign of weakness. But I think it's a sign of strength, don't you, preacher?"

Pastor Robbins stuffed the damp tissue into his pocket.

"I'll be in my office, sister Zilphia," he said. "Come and make yourself comfortable."

Zilphia hung onto the pew and watched her pastor leave the sanctuary. She had almost made up her mind that Pastor Robbins was not the one who had left the plaque on her porch, but she wanted to ask him anyway. He was a good man with a good heart and she would not be surprised if he were the mysterious woodcarver. But, after her recent roadside visit with Ray Fulcher, she had formulated another theory.

She gave Pastor Robbins what she considered to be a reasonable amount of time to compose himself. Then, she hobbled to his office and knocked on the door, which was already ajar.

"Come in," Pastor Robbins said.

"Thank you, preacher," Zilphia said, poking her head into the door.

"Please, Zilphia, sit down, and please leave the door open."

She made her way to the chair across from the pastor's desk.

"This old cancer has slowed me considerably," she said. "But I'm grateful to the Lord for the energy I have to drive my car and visit my pastor once a week."

The chair cushion hissed quietly as it accepted her frail body.

"What's on your mind, Zilphia?" Pastor Robbins said. "You're looking well and you seem to have a good amount of strength today."

"Yes, preacher, I'm doing OK today. Still very weak, you know, but, like I said, thankful to be getting about. The doctor says I am in a minor remission, that this happens sometimes to people with the kind of cancer I have, and that it could last a few days, or maybe a few weeks, but he just can't say for sure."

"Yes, that's good, Zilphia, real good. Praise the Lord"

"I try to, preacher, I really try, but it's hard, real hard."

"Try to what, Zilphia?"

"Praise the Lord. You know, what you just said."

"Oh, yes. Praise the Lord."

"Are you OK, preacher Robbins?"

"Uh, yes, Zilphia. I'm fine."

"Well, anyway, preacher, I didn't come here to talk about my sickness. We've talked that subject to death anyway, no pun intended." She giggled and the sound was like a kitten in trouble. "I just wanted to come here to thank you for what you did for me the other day."

"Thank me for what, Zilphia?"

"For the beautiful plaque you left on my doorstep, inside the newspaper. It really is a wonderful gift, and it helped me a lot. I've placed it in my kitchen, on the counter between my microwave oven and canister set. That way I can see it when I'm preparing my meals. It is such a blessing to me. But you should have knocked on the door and come in that day. I was up earlier than usual. It would have been nice to see you in person."

Pastor Robbins searched his memory.

"Zilphia, I'm sorry, but I don't know what you're talking about. Please forgive me."

"The plaque, preacher. The wooden plaque you gave me. You know, it has Romans 8:28 carved on it, and the vines and beautiful flowers. It's so beautiful, and it has helped me so much."

"I'm sorry, Zilphia. I didn't leave a plaque on your front doorstep. I wish I had, for it seems to be a gift that's really blessed you. But it wasn't me."

"But who could it have been, preacher? Who would do such a nice thing for me if it wasn't you?"

Pastor Robbins stood.

"Wait a minute, Zilphia," he said. "I think you and I have something in common. Just sit right there."

Pastor Robbins walked to the bookshelves on the wall opposite his desk. He retrieved an object from the shelf and brought it back and placed it on the desk in front of Zilphia. She studied the object.

"Why, that's very nice, preacher," Zilphia said. "It's a little church with a steeple and everything.

And there's a little man, a little preacher, with a Bible in his hand, and he's walking away from the church. It's beautiful, preacher. Where did you get it?"

"I don't know where I got it. I came into my study one evening about two weeks ago to work on my sermon and there it was, right in the middle of my desk. I've been asking around and no one admits to have given it to me, and no one knows how it got here. It's a beautiful carving, don't you think?"

"Oh, yes. It's as beautiful as my plaque. But, wait a minute. Do you think…"

"That the same person who gave you the plaque also gave me this carving? I think that might be a logical assumption."

Pastor Robbins and Zilphia studied the small carving on the desk and did not speak for what seemed a long time.

"Preacher."

"Yes Zilphia?"

"I keep looking at that little church and at that little preacher and I keep wondering the same thing over and over."

"And what's that?"

"The preacher is walking away from the church. Where in the world is he going?"

A lump rose in Pastor Robbins's throat, and he was thankful that Zilphia could not see it.

"You know, Zilphia," he said, swallowing hard. "I keep looking at that little wooden preacher and I keep wondering the same thing."

"Maybe that preacher is you," Zilphia said.

"Me? I don't know about that, Zilphia. It does kind of favor me, now that you mention it."

"Maybe someone is trying to tell you that it's time for you to move on."

"Move on? That's, well, that's not something I've considered. Until, well, until lately, but..."

"Pastor."

"Yes, sister Zilphia."

"Can I pray for you?"

"Pray for me? But, I'm the, er, I'm the pastor. You're not supposed to pray for me. I'm supposed to pray for you."

"Now, do you really believe that, preacher?"

"I, I guess not."

"You are my pastor, this is true," she said. "But you're my brother in the Lord first."

Zilphia stood and placed her hand on the corner of the desk to steady herself. She walked slowly around the desk and laid her hands on Pastor Robbins's head. He was surprised at the warmth in her hands.

"Lord," she said. "This is your servant Zilphia, and your servant Joseph. You know our hearts,

Lord, and for that we are grateful. I pray for Joseph, Father, for his spirit which is troubled. He's got a mighty weight on his shoulders, being a preacher in this old hard-headed church of yours. I ask you to take this weight from him, dear Jesus, and put it on your shoulders, which you promised you would do if we asked you to. You've got a plan for this man, my brother. Show him what it is and then give him the courage to do whatever it is you want him to do. I thank you, Lord, for Pastor Joe listening to all my griping and complaining and all my plain talk. He's been a blessing to this old dying lady. Sometimes I feel like you sent him to Dogwood just for me. Bless him, Lord, and show him the way. I know you'll do it, Lord. I know you will. Thank you, Father. Amen."

CHAPTER 13

Marie closed the post office door behind her, put the large key in the lock and turned it. She scanned the loading dock, the parking lot, the alley beyond the lot.

"There," she said. "Secure for another night."

She strolled across the parking lot and turned toward the setting sun for the two-block walk to her home. She squinted as her eyes met the bright orange blaze of the sun, lingering just at the top of the line of oak trees behind the parsonage at Dogwood Community Church. The color and angle of sunlight brought to her mind a flood of scenery, a river of memories, and on that river floated the face of her father. For it was on a day like this, in the light of a bright orange sun, that she last saw him.

She tried to turn off the memory, to dam the waters of this particular river, but neither the sunset nor the remembrance would leave. Many years had passed since she last heard the deep, strong voice of Robert Parker. Tears filled her eyes as she recalled the conversation that had become a hot brand on her soul.

"I won't be gone long," he told her. "I just need to get away for a while."

"But dad, you haven't told me where you're going."

"I don't really know, Marie. I just know I have to get away. I keep thinking of your mother, and I can't get her out of my mind. I'm angry that she's dead, and I'm heart broken, and I just don't know what to do."

Marie remembered her father's tear-streaked face, how she felt that day, how her heart had beaten in her chest like a drum, how she could not understand her father's insistence on leaving. She thought of the stories he had told her of Taylorsville, the town of his birth. In Taylorsville, he had spent a wild youth. He had been a drinker, a womanizer. It was from that place that her mother had "rescued" him. He told Marie many times of the love her mother had for him, and how that love had transformed him from a person bent on destruction to a man with a purpose. After her death, he insisted that this purpose had been jerked from him, like a hand jerked from a fire.

"Dad, you must tell me," she said. "Are you going back to Taylorsville?"

"I don't know, Marie. I just know that I have to get away."

"But what about your job, dad? What about your life here? What about me?"

"I'm not worried about you, Marie. Your Aunt Jeanette will take good care of you. You're smart and pretty and you'll go far in life. You're strong-willed and you don't let people bully you. As for my job, I've resigned. As for my life in Dogwood, I have no life here without your mother."

Then, Robert Parker got into his car and drove out of town on the Petersboro Road, heading directly into the setting sun, which blazed orange at the top of the same old oak trees.

Marie moved in with Aunt Jeanette, her mother's sister, and after many months of mourning, she and Aunt Jeanette began to mold a life together. Over the years, Marie came to see Jeanette as more of a mother than an aunt. Then, only four years ago, the same cancer that had taken her mother sneaked into the large house at the corner of Main and Stanley streets and invaded the body of Aunt Jeanette. In a few months, Aunt Jeanette passed to heaven, leaving Marie with no immediate family.

Now, as Marie pondered all these things, her anger toward her father returned. She could feel only bitterness when she remembered the man who had abandoned her, the man she had not set eyes upon since his sudden departure so many years ago.

"And where are you going this fine day, Marie Parker?"

The dry-leaf voice of Thora Langdon startled Marie.

"Oh, Ms. Thora?"

"You've been in the clouds again, young lady," Thora said, laughing. "You've walked right past your own front door."

Marie turned and saw that she had indeed walked past her own house.

"You think too much, Marie," Thora said. "I don't understand you young folks. How do you get anything done in life?"

"I just had something on my mind, I guess," Marie said, now laughing with Thora. "How dumb is it to walk past your own front door?"

"Not dumb," Thora said. "Just something that young folks aren't supposed to do. Maybe for an old bag like me, or a toddler like my little great-grand-son, Jason, but not you. What great thing were you thinking that made you lose your bearings?"

Marie did not want to tell her neighbor that she had been thinking of her father. Thora Langdon's nose was as long as Pinochio's and was always poking into places where it shouldn't poke. Marie's private thoughts were her own and no one else's. But she knew if she did not tell Thora something, the old lady would brew up her own idea of what had been going through Marie's mind, and this would not do.

"I was thinking of, well, I was thinking about a conversation I just had with Chief Norris," Marie said.

"Chief Norris? Are you in trouble with the law, young lady?"

"No, Ms. Thora, nothing like that."

"Well, what then? Come up here on the porch and tell me. I need a good story. You know how boring life is for an old lady—well, maybe you don't—but I can tell you it's boring. A good story should perk me right up. Especially a Marie Parker story."

Thora laughed again and coughed into a handkerchief. Marie stepped up to the porch.

"Here, sit in this rocking chair," Thora said. "Just put that pad and pencil on the wicker table there. I've been working on my history book a little today. The chair's clean. You won't dirty your nice pants."

Marie picked up the yellow pad and pencil and placed them on the wicker table under the picture window. She sat in the wicker chair.

"I didn't know you were writing a book, Ms. Thora," Marie said.

"Oh, yes," Thora said. "My grandchildren keep encouraging me to write a history of Dogwood based on my recollections of my grandfather, James J. Parker, who founded the town in 1880. I tell them some of these stories from time to time and they like them so much I figured somebody else might like them too."

"It's a good idea," Marie said. "People will like it. No one's ever written a history of the town before. But why don't you get a computer. It's faster than a pad and pencil."

"My son, Parker, you know him Marie. Well, he told me he would get me a computer to write with and that it would save me time and also keep me from getting writer's cramp," Thora said. "But I told him I didn't want a computer because it's something that's just too modern for me.

"Parker and his wife, Rene, and my daughter, Rachel, and her husband, Bud, they wanted to get me central heat and air one time and I told them the same thing then. And I also had to tell them not to get me a clothes dryer and a microwave oven, and I told them that cable TV was just more channels of nothing."

"I don't have cable either," Marie said.

"I'm 82 years old and I don't need to start learning how to use modern gadgets.," Thora said. "I'm OK without those things and I'm OK with a yellow legal pad and a Number 2 pencil. If the Lord had wanted me to use all those modern gizmos, he would have let me be born in 1960 and not in 1920."

Normally, Marie would have already politely bowed out of this kind of conversation with her talkative neighbor. She loved Ms. Thora, and she appreciated the small gifts of food that Ms. Thora would sometimes leave on her doorstep, and the old lady's vigilance in watching Marie's house as well as her own for what she called "riff-raff and suspicious goings-on." But today Marie welcomed the chatter, for it helped take her mind off the troubling thoughts of her father.

"Anyway," Thora said. "The stories I'm writing down are from my memory and from what was told to me by my grandfather. I'm not a writer, but I believe I can jot down a few things that might interest people here in Dogwood and maybe even in Petersboro, where James J. Parker grew up. Who knows? If I sell enough copies maybe I could get on one of them afternoon talk shows on television and then no telling what might happen."

"You might get famous," Marie said. "And rich."

"I've seen stranger things," Thora said.

Thora Langdon hushed then. She turned her eyes toward the street and stared at the dogwood tree next to the fire hydrant at the corner. Marie tried to see what her elderly neighbor was seeing, but the bold orange sunset seemed to block out everything else.

"What's it like anyway?" Thora said.

"Excuse me?" Marie said.

"Wearing pants, I mean. Rachel keeps wanting to buy me some pants, 'cause I get chilly most of the time, even in summer, but I told her I've never worn men's clothes and I don't aim to start now."

"Well, it's just like wearing anything else, I guess," Marie said.

Thora stared at the dogwood tree again. She shook her head.

"Well, Marie," she said. "Are you going to tell me what's going on or are you going to stare at that sunset all day? It's getting a little chilly out here and I'll have to go in soon. Bad circulation, you know."

"I'm sorry, Ms. Thora."

Marie related to Thora the things she had told Chief Norris about the stolen dogs. Thora listened intently, nodding her head.

"So, you think Ray Fulcher is stealing dogs?"

"Yes, I do, Ms. Thora. It just makes sense."

"Do you even know Ray Fulcher, Marie?"

"Well, I don't really know him personally, but I've delivered mail to his house for a long time, and I've seen the dogs out there and, well, he's a hermit, living in the swamp, and it just makes sense."

Thora crossed her arms and glared at Marie.

"Just because he lives in the swamp doesn't make him a hermit and just because he has dogs doesn't make him a dog thief," she said.

"It's not just the dogs, Ms. Thora. Like I was saying, he lives out there in the swamp all by himself, hardly ever coming to town. And when he does come to town, he doesn't stay long. It's like he hates people. It only makes sense to me that he's hiding something, and maybe even running from something. I'll bet he's hiding from his family. He probably left them behind somewhere, abandoned them, left them alone to fend for themselves. It's probably been twenty years since he's talked to his family. I'll bet they don't even know he's still alive!"

"Marie! What's gotten into you, girl? You're raving like a wild woman. What's Ray Fulcher ever done to you?"

Marie realized she had stepped through the gate of a kind of invisible fence and was now trespassing in territory Thora knew nothing about. She had said too much. She stood and Thora offered her handkerchief.

"No thanks," Marie said. She wiped her eyes with a sleeve. "I'm sorry, Ms. Thora. I've got to go. I need to study some materials for the post office. I got my promotion, you know. I'm sorry."

Marie hurried off Thora Langdon's porch. In a few seconds, Thora heard Marie's front door slam.

Thora rocked in her chair a few more minutes. She coughed again into her handkerchief.

"That sure beats the gossip column in The Gazette," she said.

She frowned and rocked her chair and stared again at the fire hydrant on the corner.

"I don't understand young people today. They simply have too much on their minds."

She picked up the yellow pad and pencil.

"Now, where was I?"

CHAPTER 14

Zilphia scratched the big German shepherd's head and stepped onto Ray Fulcher's front porch. A floorboard squeaked and a small dog started yapping his head off inside the house. Before she could make her shaking hand into a fist to knock on the door, Ray opened it.

"Zilphia Lassiter," Ray said. "What brings you—"

"I need to talk to you, Ray," she said.

"Um, OK, Zilphia. Come on in the house."

"No. We can talk out here on the porch. It won't take long."

Ray pushed the screen door open and Zilphia stepped out of the way.

"Have a seat on the swing," Ray said.

"No, thank you. I'd rather just stand. Sitting makes me sore. The less I sit, the better I feel."

"OK," Ray said. "But what's the matter?"

"Nothing's the matter," she said. "Well, nothing major. I just need to say something to you."

Ray opened the screen door again and Judas shot onto the porch. He stopped barking and sniffed Zilphia's ankles.

"Judas," Ray said. "Get up on the swing."

Judas sniffed again and then jumped onto the swing. Ray sat down beside him.

"All right, Zilphia. What's on your mind?"

Zilphia turned away from Ray and walked to the other side of the porch. She pulled a small plastic grocery bag from her purse. She turned quickly to face Ray and Judas.

"I hope you'll forgive me," she said, holding the bag out to Ray.

"Forgive you for what, Zilphia?"

"For taking this from your truck."

She walked to the swing. Judas growled.

"Hush Judas," Ray said.

She laid the bag on Ray's lap. Ray opened the bag and pulled out the chisel Zilphia had taken from his truck.

"A chisel," he said. "I don't understand."

"Not just any chisel," she said. "Look at it. It's yours. I took it from your truck the other day when you were changing your tire. I was looking at it and you called my name and I panicked, I guess, and just stuffed it in my sock. Cut my ankle with it."

Ray examined the chisel.

"It looks like one of my Henry Worth chisels."

"It is yours, Ray. That's what I'm trying to tell you."

"So, why didn't you just give it to me the day you took it? I mean, I was right there and…"

" Because you startled me."

"Sorry."

"No, I'm the one who's sorry. I hope you'll forgive me for keeping it. I wasn't stealing it, you know, just, well, you know."

"Yeah," Ray said. "I know. You're forgiven."

"Good. I'm glad that's over."

"Me too."

Ray laughed. Judas understood the laugh as an invitation and crawled into Ray's lap. Zilphia fidgeted with her pocketbook. She looked across the yard toward the driveway.

"OK then," Ray said. "Now that that's over, how about I go get us some iced tea?"

"Got no time for tea," Zilphia said. "Besides, I can't drink it any more. Makes me nauseous. It ain't right not being able to drink iced tea. It's unnatural."

She turned toward the steps and then stopped. Judas growled again.

"There is one other thing," she said. "One other question. No, not a question. An observation. Something I've been thinking about."

"And what would that be?" Ray said.

"The chisel. It's a woodcarving chisel, isn't it?"

"As a matter of fact, it is."

Zilphia was still looking out across the yard.

"And anyone who uses such a chisel would be a woodcarver. Is that right?"

"I suppose so," Ray said.

"And it was in that little wooden box in your truck, so it belongs to you."

"Yes, it was in my truck."

"So it, the chisel, belongs to you."

"Yes," Ray said. "And I have a question for you, Zilphia."

"For me? OK."

"Why do I feel like I'm in a courtroom in front of some high-powered attorney fighting for my life?"

Zilphia walked down the steps grasping the rail tightly. Ray stood to help, but she waved him off. Judas's tail beat furiously against the swing slats.

"Sorry, Ray," she said. "I didn't mean to make you nervous."

"I'm not nervous. Just wondering about all the questions."

"Why are you wondering?" she said. "You know what I'm talking about."

"Maybe I don't," he said.

"And maybe you do."

Zilphia got into her car and started the engine. She rolled down her window and stuck her head out. Judas yapped.

"I'll see you later, Ray," she said. "And thanks."

"Thanks? Thanks for what?"

"The forgiveness."

"Sure," Ray said.

"And for the beautiful plaque. It's one of my favorite things in the world."

Zilphia closed the window. She backed the car into the yard, barely missing Ray's rose bushes. Judas sprang from the swing, flew off the porch, and chased Zilphia's car until it exited the driveway. He stood at the mailbox and yapped until the big blue car crested the hill at Gum Creek Bridge.

CHAPTER 15

Joseph Robbins laid his book on the nightstand, reached up, and turned off the light by the bed.

"Karen. Are you awake?"

He could hear his wife's low, steady breathing. He raised his voice a little.

"Karen. Are you awake?"

She stirred. "I am now."

"I was just wondering."

"Wondering what, Joe. If I was awake, or just wondering?"

"Well, both I guess."

"OK, sweetie. Tell me. I'm all ears."

Over the years, Karen Robbins had learned that her husband was always wondering something.

Experience had taught her that it was best to allow him to speak his mind while whatever he was thinking was fresh. Her listening was not patronizing or obligatory. She loved him and knew how his mind worked. Talking things out was good therapy for the man she loved.

"Well," he said. "I was wondering why God does some of the things he does; why he is sometimes so near and so real and then why he sometimes seems so far away. I love the Lord with all my heart, but he is seldom someone I can understand."

Karen started a yawn, but stifled it. "God is always the same, Joe. No matter what we do, he loves us. No matter where we go, he goes with us."

"I know that, sweetheart. It's just that, well, sometimes I wish he was a little clearer in his directions. I would gladly do anything he asks of me, but I often don't know exactly what that is."

Karen laid her head on her husband's shoulder. She grabbed his arm and hugged it.

"I guess that's where faith comes in," she said. "It takes faith to keep following him even though we don't know what tomorrow might bring. I know you pretty well, Joseph Robbins, and I know you always want to know for sure what the next minute will bring to you. But sometimes, in fact quite often, God wants us just to hang in there, with no particular purpose except to trust him."

He considered his wife's words. Since he first met Karen, he had been impressed with, and sometimes envious of, the simplicity of her faith. His envy had never evolved into covetousness, but he had often prayed that the Lord would grant him such pure and steadfast trust. He sometimes pondered the motives of God, but Karen had always simply trusted. Joe had come to know with certainty that the influence of his wife's simple belief had more than once rescued him from the rivers of doubt.

"You know me, Karen."

"Yes, Joe, I do."

Joe wondered if now was a good time to bring up a particular thing that had been bearing on his mind for weeks.

"I know you well enough to say this: tell me what's bugging you. Whatever it is, I can take it. Remember, I'm a preacher's wife. If I haven't already seen it or heard it or thought it, then there's something wrong with me.'

They laughed.

"So, sweetie, go ahead and get it off your chest.

"Well, OK."

He cleared his throat.

"I've been thinking lately that Dogwood isn't the place for us any more. I'm in a rut here. I know we're settled and I know how you hate to move and the kids are in school and we have friends here, but, well, I've got this feeling in my gut and I've been praying night and day for a word from the Lord and he just isn't coming through for me, and…."

Karen laid her soft hand on her husband's mouth. It smelled of fresh flowers, the scent of her hand cream.

"Sssshhh," she said. "I think I get the picture, Joe."

Karen removed her hand from her husband's mouth. Neither of them spoke for what seemed like an eternity to Joe.

"So," he said. "What do you think?"

"I don't know what to say, Joe. Except for this. I'm going to lay my head back on my pillow and I'm going to turn it toward the door, like I always do so I can hear our children if they need me, and I'm going to go to sleep, and I'm going to sleep like a baby."

"That's it?" he asked.

"Yes, darling. That's it. Except for one thing."

"And that is?

"Sometimes, Joe, you just have to jump. The Lord will lead you to the lip of a mighty waterfall and you look down and it seems the most beautiful thing in the world and at the same time you know it's the most dangerous thing in the world and God asks you as straightforward as he can to jump. And you have to decide if you're going to trust him and jump, or if you're going to not trust him and stay right where you are forever."

Karen yawned and pressed her head deeper into her pillow.

"But what about, I mean, what about the waterfall? Do you know something I don't know? Is God speaking to you and not to me? Karen?"

Karen Robbins did not hear her husband's question, for she had already drifted into a peaceful sleep.

"There you go again," he whispered. "Falling asleep with that calm assurance of yours. I guess the least I can do is try to get some sleep myself."

He punched his pillow a couple of times and lowered himself deeper into the bedcovers. He wiggled so that his backside was barely touching his wife's backside. As he closed his eyes to sleep, he could not help but feel a sense of great anticipation, and he would have traded all the theology in Christendom to know exactly what that feeling meant.

CHAPTER 16

Dawson Reynolds turned the key and his truck started. He pumped the gas and relished the deafening thunder that blasted from beneath him. He revved the engine a couple more times, put the truck in gear, and screeched onto Stanley Street. He'd paid a hard-earned $800 for the muffler and, to him, it was the most beautiful music in the world.

Sunlight, bright and white, poured through Marie's bedroom window. She bolted from the bed. She realized she had fallen asleep in the clothes she had worn to work the day before. She had come directly from Miss Thora's house into her bedroom. She had been crying. She had thrown herself onto the bed and had fallen asleep without eating supper.

"That Dawson," she said. "I'd love to get my hands on that muffler for just five minutes!"

Marie showered, put on shorts and a T-shirt, socks and sneakers. She made her hair into a pony tail. She ate a quick breakfast of buttered toast and coffee and placed the dishes in the dishwasher. She found her camera bag in the closet. She laid the bag on the kitchen table and checked its contents.

"Let's see," she said. "Camera and strap, tele-photo lens, flash. Wait, I won't need the flash. Wouldn't want to give away my position. Film. I have no film."

She zipped the bag shut, grabbed her cell phone from the charger and clipped it to the waistband on her shorts. She took her wallet from the purse on the counter and slid it into the side pocket on the camera bag. She glanced around the kitchen to make sure the toaster oven and coffee maker were turned off. She breathed deeply.

"There, that should do it."

She grabbed her keys from the counter and walked out the back door and locked it. She was surprised to see that rain had fallen during the night. A thin layer of water coated the back steps and water clung to her sneakers as she walked across the grass to her car. She looked up and was grateful that the sky was now cloudless and that the sun was burning away a thin fog that still lingered in small patches.

She parked by the newspaper racks at Ralph's 24-hour Gas and Grocery. Jim Barnes was at the register when she laid the roll of 36-exposure color film on the counter.

"You're out mighty early this morning, Marie," Jim said.

"Yeah, got some things to do."

"Must be going somewhere to take some pictures."

"That's right," she said.

"I guess you figured out that Nikon after all."

"Yep."

Jim punched the cash register keys, but he couldn't take his eyes off Marie.

"You're looking nice this morning, Marie," he said. "I bet you got a date or something."

Marie thought of the one time she had gone out with Jim. She'd been attracted to him since high school, but one date can change all that, especially when the evening turns to disaster. For weeks afterward, Jim had been fairly persistent about a second date. Marie had resisted, as she did with all the men in Dogwood who'd asked her out before and since. Finally, Jim had given up. And so had the other men, most of whom were now married. Except Jim.

"Thanks, Jim," she said, without smiling or looking at him. "You're sweet to say it."

"Just telling the truth," Jim said.

Marie gave Jim money. He gave her change and placed the film and a receipt into a small plastic bag.

"There you go, Marie," he said.

"Thanks, Jim."

Jim felt a little queasy as he watched Marie get into her car. Though he tried to get his mind on something else, he thought about their date again. He'd picked her up at her house and thought she looked nice with her hair in a ponytail and her jeans and the yellow blouse with flowers embroidered on the pocket and her white sandals. He'd asked her out several times and was happy she'd finally said yes.

"You look real nice," he'd told her.

"You too, Jim." She smiled and Jim thought his heart would tear out of his chest. "I've been wanting to see *"A Walk to Remember"* for a long time, ever since it came out."

"I heard it's kind of a girl movie," Jim said, laughing.

"Yeah, I guess so. We can see something else if you want to," Marie said.

"No. I asked you to this movie and that's the one we're going to see."

Jim thought Marie was impressed with his unselfish attitude.

"How about we go to the Chicken Shack first, get a bite to eat and then the movie?" he said.

"Sounds great. I could eat some fried chicken."

The drive to Petersboro had been pleasant enough. He and Marie had talked about many things. Her work, his work. Things going on in town.

"How's your photography going?" she asked.

"Good, real good," he said. "I was out at the creek just below the bluffs at the Grandy Field the other day. It's one of my favorite spots. The rhododendron was in bloom. I think it's amazing that wild rhododendron grows this far east. It's a mountain plant, you know."

"I didn't know that," Marie said. " Maybe we could go out there together some time. I've been tinkering with my new Nikon some lately. Maybe you could show me how to use it."

Jim had looked around the car then, to see just where his heart might have jumped to.

They talked about their high school days and wondered where the time had gone, and what had happened to some of their old friends that had moved away.

"I heard Fred Bonner's down in Taylorsville, working with Branch Bank," Jim said. "His momma said he's doing real good these days. Got a wife and kids. She said he loves it in Taylorsville."

Marie had not responded to Jim's remark about Fred Bonner or Taylorsville. In fact, she had not spoken ten words the rest of the evening. He wondered what it was about Fred Bonner that had made her clam up like she did. As soon as he'd said Fred Bonner, or maybe it was when he said Taylorsville, or maybe it was something else he said. He just couldn't figure it out.

They went to the Chicken Shack and ate in silence. They went to the movie and Marie's mind seemed to be a million miles away. She didn't even cry at the end when she was supposed to. The drive back home had been like a funeral to Jim. When he dropped Marie off at her house, she said "Thank you for a nice evening," got out of the car and went into her house and shut the door. Jim had sat in his car for a few minutes in a kind of stunned silence. Marie didn't even turn a light on in the house.

He saw her the next day at the post office and told her he'd had a nice time. He told her he was off on Wednesday and asked if she'd like to go with him to the bluffs on Gum Creek.

"No thank you, Jim," she'd said.

And that was it.

He'd spent the last few months wondering what he'd done to upset her. He thought about it every day of his life and he was miffed with himself for thinking about it now.

Marie sat in the parking lot long enough to load the film into the camera. She started the car, pushed her favorite Dolly Partin CD into the player and drove from the parking lot onto Main Street. From there, she turned right onto the Petersboro Road, and after a half mile turned left onto Gum Swamp Road. She slowed her car to a crawl, took a deep breath, and gunned the engine.

CHAPTER 17

Mushrooms? You wanna take pictures of mushrooms?"

"Yes, Mr. Elmer. I, well, I sort of like mushrooms, the way they look, and photography is a hobby of mine, and I think some nice mushroom photos would look nice in my house...."

"But it's kinda dangerous in the swamp, Miss Parker," Elmer Tarkington said. "They's snakes in there, and other things. Of course the snakes would be a little woozie this time of day, it being cool in the mornings. And they's some quicksand if you ain't careful."

"I know, Mr. Elmer. But I've been in swamps before. And I've been a hiker and camper all my life. I know how to take care of myself in the outdoors."

Elmer Tarkington lifted his cap and used the same hand to scratch the top of his head. He looked at his feet and then at Marie.

"Well, I reckon it'll be all right."

"Thanks, Mr. Elmer."

"Me and the wife, we're going to the coast today," Elmer said. "Gonna visit our grandchildren down at Topsail. Do some fishing. Be gone at least two, three days. So we won't be at the house here. Anybody else know you're going down to the swamp?"

"Uh, oh yes, Mr. Elmer."

"Well, all right then. You can drive on down to that barn next to the woods, that old tobacco barn. The one with the black tin roof."

Elmer Tarkington pointed and Marie nodded.

"The path down there is real good and solid and you won't have no trouble with your car. Just park it by the barn and you can get into the swamp that way. They's some game trails back that way. Deer mostly use it to come up to my corn and nibble now and then. That'll take you on into the woods. They might be some mushrooms back in there. They might be poking their heads up out of the ground, especially since it rained a little last night."

"That sounds perfect, Mr. Elmer. And will those trails get me to the creek?"

"Well, I reckon. Deers gotta drink water like the rest of us."

Elmer laughed.

"But be careful, girl. The rain's probably made the ground slick in right many places. Make sure you step cautious. And remember, if you smell cucumbers, stop walking and turn around and go a different route cause that's a copperhead. He'll put out a scent like cucumbers when he's disturbed, and he ain't afraid of anything and he's the only snake I know of that'll stand his ground and not run from a man, or a woman. And if he bites you its bad news."

Marie did not fear snakes, but the thought of a copperhead bite did muster a small shiver. She instinctively checked her waist for the cell phone.

"Oh, I'll be careful, Mr. Elmer. I've got my phone so I can call rescue if something happens. But I don't think anything will go wrong. I won't be in there long anyway. Just long enough for a few photographs."

"All right then. We'll probably be gone when you come back out. I'm out here waiting for Jean right now. She's calling Aaron, telling him we're on the way down there. Course, when Jean gets on the phone they ain't no tellin' how long she'll be."

Elmer laughed again and Marie chuckled with him.

"Well, I'll be on my way," Marie said. "Thanks again, Mr. Elmer."

"You're certainly welcome, Miss Parker. And please be careful."

"I will. Don't worry about that. And have a nice time at Topsail."

Marie entered the woods on a game trail behind the old tobacco barn. She thought of snakes. She remembered Tom Jenkins, a farmer who lived near Benton, on the Petersboro side of Gum Swamp. A couple of years earlier, Jenkins killed a large rattle-snake while hunting turkeys with his eight year-old son. According to Jenkins' account in the Petersboro Herald, the rattler measured six feet four inches long from snout to rattle. The snake was sunning by the water at the Big Rock, near the mouth of Gum Creek. Jenkins killed the snake with his shotgun and carried it to town, where a Herald photographer snapped the photo that many folks in Smith County still talk about.

"But that was on the other side of the swamp, near the Big Rock, near boulders and other stuff that rattlesnakes love. I'm not likely to find one this far south."

She made her way carefully down the trail and into a thicket of wax myrtles. She picked up her pace a little when she caught a scent of dampness. She knew she was nearing the creek. She stopped, swatted a large mosquito from her arm, and checked her camera bag. She made sure her cell phone was still in its place on her waist. She craned her neck and squinted through the thick woods and undergrowth, searching in the direction of Ray Fulcher's house.

"I know it's that way," she said. "Just a little more and I should be able to see it. I can't wait to see Chief Norris's face when I show him the pictures. He'll see that I'm right about that old hermit."

CHAPTER 18

Marie bent over to re-tie her shoe. The lace had snagged on a catbriar and had pulled loose as she stepped over a small log. It was a small thing, but another frustration among several she had endured over the last hour. She found a dry spot among the mostly wet forest floor and sat down. She wanted to get her bearings, to find some kind of landmark, to figure out just where she was and how she was going to get back out to the road. She prided herself on being an intelligent, modern woman who could figure most things out without help from anyone. She needed only a few minutes to sit awhile and clear her mind of all distractions.

She remembered Elmer Tarkington's words of warning and the stories she'd heard about Gum Swamp. Neither produced the slightest fear. In her mind, she retraced her steps.

She had entered the swamp on the east side of the creek. She'd walked in sight of the road to within a couple hundred yards of Ray Fulcher's mailbox and she'd turned sharply to the north, into the heart of the swamp. She had intended to swing to the backside of Ray's house, snap a few photographs, circle around to her starting point, get into her car, and head back to town. The plan was simple, but its execution had become more complex by the minute. The snag was the swamp itself. She had not imagined how easily someone might get confused in the tangle of trees and vines and underbrush.

She sat on damp leaves, sweating, thirsty, and nearly exhausted. She had not brought food or water, thinking that she would be in the swamp an hour at the most. Mosquitoes dined on her bare arms and legs. Why had she worn shorts and a T-shirt? Why had she not brought water and insect repellent? Why had she not let Chief John Norris do the investigating? That was, after all, his profession. Why was she always doing impulsive things like this? Why was she so strongly drawn to that man living in that old house in Gum Swamp?

Marie stood and wiped the perspiration from her brow as well as she could with the back of her sweaty hand. She negotiated the briars and vines, searching intently for a landmark, a building, a barn, the creek, anything to give her an inkling of where she was. She listened for a car engine, a train, any noise that might indicate how far she might have traveled from the road. Birds chirped and sang in the tall gums and maples. Now and then, the wind grabbed tree limbs and rubbed them together in an eerie moan. The muck of Gum Swamp soaked her sneakers, her socks, her feet.

"Come on, girl. You can make it," she said, breathing heavily. "You're not really lost. Just a little disoriented. How big can this horrible swamp be anyway? Just keep walking. Keep your eyes on the ground, on your feet. What time is it anyway?"

Marie looked at her watch. In this one brief act of inattention, her left foot caught a large vine that had hidden itself among graceful ferns. She felt herself falling. She instinctively reached her arms out, searching for something to grab, something to break the fall. But there was no branch, no tree, no shrub. Only empty air. Her camera and bag flew from around her neck.

She hit the ground hard. Her teeth clamped like a vise and pain shot through her jaw. She reached out again but caught only a handful of damp leaves. She tumbled, rolling over and over on the forest floor. She heard a sharp crack, like a dry stick breaking. Indescribable pain shot through her left leg and she screamed and her scream echoed through the cavern of tall trees. She realized she was toppling down a steep slope, rolling over saplings and small brush, ferns and reeds.

Then, the tumbling stopped and Marie lay still.

When she awoke, Marie did not remember where she was.

A deep fear grabbed her as she tried to understand why she was lying in a pile of damp leaves, why she could not move, why her body seemed filled from head to toe with pain, why the world around her had become so cloudy. She recalled the swamp, walking, tripping, and then the slightest recollection of falling, of tumbling, pain, and, then, a kind of smoky darkness.

She tried to rise. Pain pinched her leg, then the rest of her body like tweezers. Her eyes filled with tears and the tears rolled down her cheeks and into the corner of her mouth. She gritted her teeth. She tried to shift her weight from the injured leg, to rise by pushing herself up with her hands and arms. But this motion only fed the pain. She searched for a stick or tree limb, anything that might help her get to her feet. She saw her camera and bag and one of her shoes. These things had torn away from her during the fall. A gully, a ravine of sorts rose around and above her. She tried to remember how she had managed to get herself into such a situation. The ravine was at least five or six feet deep. Why had she not seen it?

She lay her head onto the soft leaves. Her mind seemed locked, frozen. She could not think. She was ashamed at her own foolish audacity, at having been so stubborn as to try to negotiate Gum Swamp alone. Elmer Tarkington's words of warning ran through her mind. She wished that she had not been so hard-headed. She wished that she had listened to Elmer, a man who knew this land well, who had lived on it all his life, who was wiser than she.

She felt for her cell phone. It wasn't on her waistband. It wasn't within sight on the ground. Muscles in the back of her neck tightened as she understood how vulnerable she was. She sniffed for the scent of cucumbers, the tell-tale sign of the copperhead. She smelled only musky, wet leaves, the spicy aroma of cypress and cedar.

She pictured Elmer Tarkington and his wife driving happily along the interstate highway toward Topsail Island. She thought of Jim Barnes at the store and Thora Langdon rocking on her porch.

And she wished she had told someone else where she was going.

CHAPTER 19

Chief John Norris watched with delight as his thirty or so bantam chickens lapped up their food.

"That's right boys and girls. Eat up. The fair's in five weeks. We want you fat and sassy by then."

He could not help the pride he felt for his small brood of chickens. He'd been raising bantams since he was a boy and he owned several blue ribbons to prove his prowess as a breeder of prizewinners. He loved raising chickens and he took great pleasure in coming out to the old home place every day to feed them and watch over them. Though he'd lived in town for twenty years, he still found the air of the country to his liking. But more than the chickens and country air, he cherished the solitude, the time to himself.

"You guys are looking good. Real good. If I can keep that old fox away from you, we'll bring some more ribbons home this year."

He tossed a handful of feed on the ground and thought about Marie's dog-thief theory. He thought about the dogs he saw in Ray Fulcher's truck. He watched his chickens peck the ground.

"You guys are like me," he said. "The feed is all over the place. You peck and peck and sometimes you get feed and sometimes you get dirt. No matter how hard you try, you always pick up dirt with the feed. I'm trained to separate the feed from the dirt, the truth from fiction. But all I'm doing is pecking the ground like you.

"Ray Fulcher is a little weird; a strange man, but one who never gives anyone any trouble. He tends to his own business, a rare trait in Dogwood. He comes to town every now and then, always with a wave of the hand, always with a smile. And always with a truckload of dogs. Even before the dog thefts, Ray carried dogs around in his truck.

"But I never noticed them before now," he said, tossing another handful of feed onto the ground. "I wish I had. I'm trained to notice things. But I don't really notice anything. Some detective I've turned out to be. Some chief of police. Miss Adams is right about me."

The chickens clucked happily and pecked the ground. Chief Norris remembered the day last August when he arrived at the barn to find one of his prize roosters dead in the pen. He'd examined the bird carefully. It had been bleeding from several puncture wounds on its head. He's seen it before. When one chicken is injured slightly, the others will gather around it and start pecking at the wound. They'll continue this cruel ritual until the injured chicken is dead, killed by its own kind.

"Sometimes I think some of the people in this town are like you chickens," he said. "They find a weakness in somebody, something they don't like, some suspicion of wrongdoing, and they peck that person to death. If these folks get wind of Marie's theory about the dogs, they'll never let up on me, or on Ray Fulcher, until I look into it."

Marie Parker was a busybody, of course. Chief Norris had known her father and mother years earlier, but he'd not thought of them in a long while. He had known Marie as long as he could remember. She was a Dogwood native, like him, though he figured she was at least 10, maybe 15 years younger. She was smart enough to land the job at the post office and to get her promotion to postmistress, and she handled that job with a great amount of proficiency. He'd never heard any complaints about the post office, except the occasional snippet about Marie's nosiness and her sometimes snappy attitude. But she'd never done or said anything to him to make him think she was less than intelligent and professional.

"But I can't just go on what she's told me," he said. "I'm a law enforcement officer and she's just the postmistress. There's no evidence that Ray's the dog thief. But, then again, there's no proof that he's not."

He tossed the last handful of feed at the chickens. They rushed to the spot, fighting each other for the best morsels.

"There's only one thing to do," he said. "When there's a lack of evidence, you go out searching for some. You go to the place where the evidence is likely to be. And in this case, it's Ray Fulcher's house. If you find something out there that warrants an arrest, or further investigation, then you do your sworn duty. If you don't find anything, you look somewhere else. You keep looking and digging, you keep pecking until you pick up the feed."

The rude chirping of a cell phone invaded the chief's happy solitude.

"I wished I'd left that thing at home."

The phone's screen displayed his home phone number.

"Hello Martha."

"John, are you coming back any time soon? I'm leaving in about an hour for church. If you're going, you need to come on back and get ready."

He had forgotten that it was Sunday.

"No, I don't think I'm going today. Got too much on my mind."

"On your mind? What in the world would keep your mind so occupied that you couldn't sit for a couple hours in Sunday school and church?"

"I'm thinking about the dogs, Martha. The stolen dogs. I know it's a minor thing, but I've got this theory and, well, I need to look into it."

"You just want to stay out there with your chickens."

"Well, it's probably a little of that too, sweetie."

Martha laughed. She had lived with her husband long enough to know that he loved his work, and his chickens. When both of them needed attention, she usually took a back seat, though she was quite happy with the attention he gave to her. She often wished he would be more serious about church, about the Lord's work, but she had no complaints about him as a husband. She considered him her best friend and a good partner in life. She thanked the Lord often for her blessed life and she prayed each day that the Father would keep her husband out of harm's way.

"Sometimes John Norris, I think you love your chickens more than you love me."

"You know that's not true."

"All right then. I've talked to Momma and she wants us to go over there after church for lunch. I'll just meet you there. How's that sound?"

"Sounds great to me. What's she having?

"Fried chicken. Bantams."

John chuckled.

"Very funny," he said. "I'll see you there."

"Bye."

John placed the phone back into its holster. He spread a scoop of chicken feed on the ground, closed the gate on the pen and walked toward his car, wiping his shoes on the grass.

"I'll see you fellows tomorrow," he said. "Sunday or not, I've got work to do."

CHAPTER 20

The little bell on the door tinkled like coins in a glass jar. John Norris let the door close behind him. He joined his friend, Boyd, in the booth in the corner by the milk and juice cooler. He moved disheveled newspapers from the seat and placed them on the table in the next booth over. He waved at Hazel, who was counting money at the register. She finished counting, got a Hazel's Grill cup from the shelf near the coffee pot, filled the cup and sat it on the table in front of the chief.

The chief sipped the coffee, pulled a napkin from the holder, folded it and laid it on the table, and sat the cup on the napkin.

"Hey Hazel," he said. "Where's my cup?"

"Sorry, chief. Hank broke it at the sink. Dropped it on his steel-toed shoes."

"That was my Sheriff's Association cup. I got it at the convention last year. I loved that cup."

"I said I'm sorry. I can't help it if Hank can't hold onto a silly old cup. Besides, you can't tell me the coffee don't taste just as good in my cup."

Boyd looked up from his newspaper and said, "I can't tell you the coffee tastes good in any cup."

"You ain't got to drink it," Hazel said.

"I do if it's the only coffee in town on Sunday morning," Boyd said.

"If you'd go ahead and take a drink of that bad coffee maybe it would stop your bad mouthing," Hazel said.

"All right, children, that's enough," Chief Norris said. He and Boyd laughed and Hazel went into the back room.

Chief Norris sipped his coffee again.

"It bothers me a little, Boyd, enough to make me wonder if Marie is right," he said.

"Right about what?"

"The dogs, Boyd, the dogs. If your memory was a car it would never crank."

Chief Norris had seen Boyd at the auction the night before and had spent more than a few minutes relating Marie Parker's theory about Ray Fulcher's dogs.

"Oh, oh yeah, the dogs."

John Norris loved his old friend, but sometimes he believed Boyd was getting a little senile, even at 55.

"Sorry, John, I got my mind on the newspaper here. Just trying to get this last word in the Jumble. It's a tough one. Go ahead, tell me again."

Boyd laid his pen on the table.

"As I told you last night, Marie Parker thinks Ray Fulcher is the one stealing all the breed dogs around town. She goes out to Ray's every day on her mail route, or at least she used to before Nell took over. She says it seems to her that there's more dogs out there every time she goes by. And she said every now and again she's seen several cars parked in Ray's yard, like there's a gathering of some kind. She thinks Ray's stealing the dogs and then either fighting them or selling them."

"I don't know about that," Boyd said. "The hermit's kinda strange and likes to keep to himself, but he's a nice enough fellow. I saw him just yesterday at the hardware store. He waved at me and told me to have a nice day. I don't know if he'd be stealing dogs."

Chief Norris remembered seeing Ray, and a truckload of dogs, at the hardware store.

"You may be right," John said. "But Marie's argument has a ring of truth about it. I feel it in my gut."

"What I feel in my gut is Hazel's sausage," Boyd said, pointing to his biscuit. "I think she actually got the syringe out this morning and injected pure old pig grease into this batch. Hey, that's it. G-R-E-A-S-E. That's the last Jumble word!"

Boyd picked up his pen and scribbled the word into the appropriate blocks on the Jumble puzzle.

"Now let's see if I can figure out the surprise answer. I love the Jumble, don't you, John?"

John jerked the pen from Boyd's hand and placed it in his own shirt pocket.

"Now what'd you do that for?"

"Boyd, I'm trying to tell you something here."

"OK, I'll listen. But would you give me back my pen when you're done?"

Hazel came out of the back room carrying a small crate of cabbages. Chief Norris waved at her and pointed to his coffee cup. He repeated his concerns about Ray Fulcher and the missing dogs. He told Boyd that he, too, had seen Ray Fulcher the day before, while he was parked at the hardware store.

"Yes, I just told you that's where I saw him," Boyd said.

"I know," Chief Norris said. "But did you notice what was in the back of his truck?"

"Actually, I did. He had several large bags of dog food, and several large dogs. In fact, I'd say he had at least one dog per bag, or one bag per dog, however you want to look at it."

Boyd laughed again.

"I'm serious," Chief Norris said. "Did you notice what kinds of dogs he had in his truck?"

"Well, the usual ones, I guess. I didn't really think about it. Ray's been coming to town since he moved here, and he always brings three or four dogs with him. I never noticed what kinds they are, though. Just dogs. Mangy-looking dogs, but plain old dogs."

"I saw the truck as I was walking from the post office back to town hall," Chief Norris said. "In my line of work, I'm not supposed to jump to conclusions without evidence, but I could have sworn there was a German shepherd in that truck, and a golden Lab, and maybe even a bulldog. That's three of the dogs that have been reported missing."

"Well, John, you just might have something. But, if Ray stole those dogs, why would he bring them to town in his truck for everyone to see? You're the police officer, though. You're trained in detecting."

Boyd took a sip from his coffee.

"Just do me one favor," he said.

"And what's that, Boyd?"

"Just remember the source of your information. Marie happens to be the biggest busybody in town. And the nosiest, except for Thora Langdon. You know how Marie likes to talk. I don't know if I'd take much stock in her theories."

"I know it seems a little odd, me being a professional and taking theories from a civilian. But, like I said, there's something about it that doesn't add up."

John took Boyd's pen from his pocket and handed it to his friend.

"Here, finish your Jumble. I've got somewhere I need to be."

"And where would that be?"

"I think I'll just take a little drive over to Gum Swamp Road."

"But it's Sunday, John. Why don't you give it a rest until tomorrow. Stick around and help me finish the Jumble. Besides, Ray's house is outside your jurisdiction."

"A sworn law officer doesn't know one day from another, Boyd. Sunday's a work day for me, just like any other. And it won't hurt a thing for me to take a look out there at Ray's place. If I see anything worthwhile, I'll call Sheriff Newsome for backup."

"Backup? Are you gonna call the SWAT team on poor old Ray and his mangy dogs?"

Boyd laughed again.

"Laugh if you want. I'm going to the house and put on my uniform. Then I'm going out to Ray Fulcher's."

Chief Norris placed a dollar on the table. Hazel was there to claim it before he could stand up.

"Thanks, Chief, come on back again tomorrow now," Hazel said.

"Thanks, Hazel. I'll see you guys around. And, by the way, Hazel. Your coffee tastes the same in your cup as it did in mine."

"See, Boyd," Hazel said. "The chief likes my coffee."

"He said it tasted the same in either cup," Boyd said. "He didn't say he liked it."

Hazel slapped Boyd gently on the shoulder and they watched Chief John Norris walk out the door.

"Hazel, that John Norris sure is dedicated," Boyd said. "And about as naïve as they come."

But Hazel had not heard him. She was already in the back of the restaurant, dialing the phone.

CHAPTER 21

Gertrude Tingle crushed her cigarette into the ashtray and opened the oven door. The heat slapped her face and she turned quickly away. She grabbed a dish towel and pulled the baking sheet from the oven and slammed the sheet onto the counter. She took a large platter from the cabinet and lifted each biscuit with her thumb and forefinger and placed them onto the platter. She carried the platter into the dining room and sat it in the center of the table. She performed this chore methodically, as she had done every morning for the last 22 years.

Robert Parker was already at the table, as were Bill Fisk and Roberta Miller.

"Where's Johnny?" she asked the others. "If he don't stop being late for breakfast, I'm gonna stop fixing it for him."

"In the bathroom," Bill said. "Can't nobody get in there 'cause of him being in there so long. I think you ought to build another bathroom, Trudy. It would sure help out around here. One bathroom ain't enough for four people, five counting yourself."

"And tell me, Mr. Fisk, where I'm gonna get the money to build another bathroom," Gertrude said. "I could raise your rent. That would probably do it."

"Not a good idea," Bill said. "Rent's too much already."

"Eighty dollars a month is a fair rent," Gertrude said. "And if all of you would pay it on time, I might could do some improvements around here."

Gertrude glared at Robert Parker, who sat at the head of the table, his head hung like a hurt dog.

"What do you think about that, Robert Parker?" Gertrude said. "Some people need to catch up on their rent."

Robert looked at Gertrude and his gloomy eyes made her wish she'd not chastised him in front of the others. In the 20 years that he'd lived in her boarding house, he'd paid his rent faithfully, though his job history reminded her of the movements of a yo-yo. He'd not paid her in three months, since he lost his job at the lumber mill, but she'd not said anything about it until now.

"You know I haven't worked in a while, Trudy," he said.

"Yeah, I know that, Robert. But I also don't see you trying to get a job either. I can't keep feeding somebody that doesn't pay the room rent."

"Sorry, Trudy," Robert said. "I'll try harder."

Gertrude Tingle had opened her home for boarders a few months after her husband's death. Her husband, a small man with a large laugh, walked out into the street one day to get the morning paper, tripped on the curb, and fell onto a fire hydrant. The blow to his head left him in a coma for six days. On the seventh day, he died. Gertrude had never quite gotten over his passing, and the fact that he had no life insurance, no pension, no nothing to support her. She received a Social Security check each month and the money she made from her boarders. And now, Robert Parker was three months behind and she was feeling the pinch in her pocketbook.

Gertrude joined the others at the table and scooped a large spoonful of scrambled eggs onto her plate.

"I remember when you came to me wanting a place to stay, Robert," Gertrude said. "It was 20 years ago, but it seems like yesterday. Boy, were you in a mess. And, boy, was your mouth shut tighter than a cork in a bottle. You remember that, don't you, Robert?"

"Yes. I remember."

"I asked you where you were from and what you did for a living and tried to get some information from you, you know, because I didn't want to let just anybody live here, and you wouldn't tell me a thing. I just felt pure sorry for you and let you live here anyway."

"I haven't caused you any problems, Trudy," Robert said. "I've been faithful with my rent until just recently. I'll make it up to you. You know I will."

"I guess so," Gertrude said. "But three months is a long time, Robert."

"What about me?" Shirley Miller said. "I remember I went two months without paying. That was a couple years ago. Remember that Trudy?"

"That I do," she said, reaching for the bacon plate.

"But I paid you all of it."

"That you did," she said.

Gertrude chewed on her bacon. Bill opened a biscuit, plopped a thick slab of butter inside and closed it. He dipped the biscuit into his coffee and bit into it.

"Good biscuit," he said. "As usual."

"Yes, Gertrude," Shirley said. "As usual."

Gertrude allowed her eyes to scan the people sitting around her table. She considered herself a sort of mother to her boarders, though all of them were well past middle age. Each one carried around the kind of baggage that would weigh down even the hardiest of souls, and though she wasn't a religious person, she felt her boarding house was a kind of mission for folks like these.

Shirley Miller showed up on her porch four years ago, on a day so cold that a polar bear would have felt at home. She had been traveling across the country, she said, in a motor home with her husband. They had pulled into a service station on the outskirts of Taylorsville to use the rest rooms and when she got out, her husband had left her there, alone and with no money. Gertrude thought the story had a few holes in it, but she allowed Shirley to move in just the same. Shirley quickly got a job at the Bobcat Grill over on Highway 96 and had been a faithful payer of her rent ever since, except for those strange two months. So, Gertrude had never asked any questions about Shirley's previous life.

Bill Fisk was a different story. A man from social services had called Gertrude and asked if she would take Bill in to stay awhile. The social services man said his office would guarantee his rent indefinitely, and she needed desperately to rent the room out, so she agreed to house Bill until better arrangements could be made. That was 12 years ago and social services was still paying Bill's rent. He worked every day at the sheltered workshop for the handicapped and was messy, but had never caused any trouble.

Then there was Robert Parker. Of all her boarders, Robert was the most mysterious. He'd come to her place only a couple of years after she opened it up for boarders. He didn't say much then and he had kept to himself, not letting anyone in on where he was from or anything else about his past life. Gertrude saw Robert as a sort of family member, maybe as a cousin or step-brother, mainly because he'd been with her so long. But she had always been curious about him. He was much smarter than any boarder she had ever had before or since. But his lips were closed tighter than a padlock.

"You got something on your mind, today, don't you Robert?" Gertrude said. "But what am I talking about? You've always got something on your mind. You've got twenty years of something on your mind. If I weren't such a nosey person, I'd leave you alone about it. But, you've sat in that chair at my table for all these years and I just realized I don't know a thing about you. Isn't that strange, Robert?"

"Strange," Bill Fisk said.

"Odd," Shirley Miller said.

"You've always been a gloomy person, Robert," Gertrude said. "But lately you've been like one of those Bassett hounds. You know, those dogs that look like they're about to cry any minute, their skin hanging off them like a bunch of old rags. That's what you remind me of."

"A Bassett hound," Bill said, laughing so hard that he spit his biscuit onto the table.

"Good grief, Bill!" Gertrude said. "Look what you've done. You're about the sloppiest eater I've ever seen."

Bill laughed again and said, "But you called him a Bassett hound, Trudy. That's funny in my book."

"Your book is full of blank pages, Bill." Gertrude said.

Shirley snickered. She took a final bite of eggs, wiped her mouth and pushed herself away from the table.

"This place is a fun house," she said. "I've got to go to work. Maybe there's some sane people at the restaurant this morning.'

"Very funny," Gertrude said.

"I've got to go, too," Robert said.

"And where would you be going, Robert?" Gertrude said. "To get a job, maybe? Or to try to find some money for rent, I hope."

"No," Robert said. "I've had enough. I've got to go home."

Gertrude was about to ask Robert what he meant by going home, but she remembered the last time he'd said the same thing. It was two weeks ago, and she had been chiding him about finding a job. He'd gotten upset and told her he was going home. When she asked him where home was, he clammed up, slammed his fork on the table, and stormed into his room. She didn't want to make the same mistake again, though in her heart she was bursting to find out what he really meant.

"Home is where the heart is, Robert," she said. "And I'd sure like to know where your heart is this morning."

"That's it," Robert said. "I'm going home."

He took his napkin from his lap and laid it on the table. He stood and walked to his room, pulled a pillow out of its case, and gathered his few belongings—a dog-eared New Testament, a silver cross on a chain, his empty wallet, and a framed photograph of a man and a woman and a little girl. He stuffed the things and his few pieces of clothing into the pillowcase. He opened his door slightly and saw that Gertrude and Bill were still sitting at the table. Gertrude was wiping up Bill's mess and Bill was still laughing. Johnny Walker came out of the bathroom down the hall and Robert closed his door until he was sure Johnny was in the dining room. He opened the door again, walked down the hall, through the kitchen, and out the back door. The morning air was cool and a little damp and he shivered and then took a deep breath. He didn't have a car. He had no money for a bus ticket. He was afraid to hitchhike.

"I guess I'll walk," he said. "It's not that far to Dogwood, maybe a day's walk, maybe two. Walking will do me good."

He took a step onto the grass just beyond the bottom step on Gertrude Tingle's back porch. He hesitated, resisted the urge to go back into the house and lock himself in his room, something he'd done many times since moving to Taylorsville. Then he took another step, and the grass felt good beneath his feet, and he imagined it to be a kind of carpet, a red carpet leading him to his ultimate destination.

Under his breath, he said a prayer. "I don't know what I'm doing, Lord. And I don't know what'll happen when I get there. But I know I got to do it. Help me do it. Help me to not turn back this time. I'm scared as I've ever been, Lord. She might throw me out on my backside, and I deserve that. But help me get all the way this time, Lord."

He walked around the old house. The peeling paint, the falling shutters, the old porch swing, all familiar things, but now, somehow, all strange things. He walked through the rickety gate and closed it until he heard it click shut. He took a few more steps away from the house, then he looked at it again, and then he walked to the corner, turned in the direction of Dogwood, and did not look back at the old house again.

CHAPTER 22

The porch swing squeaked like an old, rusty door hinge. Ray rocked gently in the swing for a few minutes, then he stood.

"Judas," he said. "I can't stand it any more. This old swing needs some relief."

The little dog yipped, happy that his master had paid him a bit of attention.

Ray walked into the house and returned a few minutes later with a can of spray lubricant. He sprayed a generous amount of the lubricant on each of the chain hooks. The oil covered the hooks and then ran down each chain. Some of it dripped onto the porch.

"Now, I've got to clean the chain and the porch," he said. "If it's not one thing, it's another."

Ray had worked hard to get his home ready for the meeting, and now, on this bright and beautiful Sunday morning, he was nit-picking. He wanted things to be as perfect as possible for his friends, and especially for Darlene. In the four months that he'd known Darlene, he'd come to have great respect for her. Like Ray, Darlene had lost her spouse to the ravages of a terminal disease. This was the first thing they had in common. She was also a lover of nature and a simple person, content to take life one day at a time, not moving around in a mad rush, not expecting any particular favors from the world, and simply abiding in the love of the Lord. Ray had been impressed from the beginning with Darlene's unwavering faith in God. She knew how to wait on the Lord, to really just do nothing until she was sure the Lord was in it. In Ray's mind, this knowing how to patiently wait for God was a spiritual achievement of the highest order. He wanted to know how to wait, and he knew Darlene could teach him this simply by her example.

He went back into the house for a handful of paper towels and the cleaner. When he returned to the porch, Judas was looking toward the driveway and barking. He was delighted to see Darlene's car pulling into the drive.

"Judas, you're making too much noise," he said. "It's just Darlene. She won't bite."

He opened the screen door and Judas went inside. He walked out to his driveway and met Darlene at her car.

"Hi Ray," she said. "You look nice this morning."

She hugged him and patted him on the back with both hands. Ray thought he might melt into the ground.

"You've been cleaning," she said.

Ray still held the papers towels and cleaner in his hands.

"Oh," he said. "No, I mean, well, I was just cleaning up a little spill on the porch. I oiled the swing chains and some of the oil got on the porch floor."

"You *are* particular, Ray Fulcher," she said, smiling. "You always want everything to be just right."

"Well, nothing but the best for you, and, er, the worship group," he said.

"Come on, then," Darlene said. "I'll help."

"No, I'll get it. You might get some of that nasty oil on your clothes. By the way, you look nice today, too."

"Thanks, Ray."

They strolled across the yard and onto the porch. Ray cleaned the oil spots from the floor and wiped off the swing chains.

"Now," he said. "Sit with me in the swing. It'll be awhile before the rest of the folks get here. Let's just sit and enjoy this beautiful Sunday morning."

"Sounds great," Darlene said.

They sat in the swing and it gently rocked them. The chain no longer squeaked against the hooks and Ray was happy about that. A gentle breeze rose from the woods and fell across the porch. A mockingbird sang in the maple tree next to the house. Ray counted seven different songs.

"You've got a nice place here," Darlene said. "So peaceful."

"Yes," Ray said. "The Lord has really blessed me. The place was kind of run down when I got it, and I spent some money fixing it up, but I'm pleased with the way it turned out. It's just right for me. Quiet, you know. Away from the crowd. Sometimes I sit out here on the porch and can hear the trains going through, whistling at the Petersboro Road crossing, and again at Main Street and then at Juniper Road. I don't know any of the engineers, of course, but I've come to sort of know them by the way they make their whistles blow. Each one is different, but always the same, if you know what I mean."

"You're very observant," she said.

"And that mockingbird," he said. "I sat on the back porch one day and counted fourteen different songs from that one bird. I suppose he's got more than that, but I just lost count at fourteen."

Darlene closed her eyes and listened to the mockingbird. She delighted in the breeze from the forest. She opened her eyes and slid closer to Ray until she was touching him. He did not move away from her.

She wanted to place her hand in his hand, but he still held the cleaner in one hand and the soiled paper towels in the other.

"You want me to get rid of that stuff for you?" she said.

"What stuff?"

"The cleaner. The paper towels. I can take them in the house for you."

"Mercy," Ray said. "I forgot...I'll take them in. You just wait right here. Promise me you won't move."

She grinned and Ray thought his heart would explode. "I'll stay right here, I promise," she said.

Ray walked to the door and then he hesitated. He turned toward the swamp. He tilted his head as he tried to discern the racket coming from deep within the forest.

"What?" Darlene said. "What is it?"

"Do you hear that?" he said.

"Hear what? All I can hear now is Judas. He's yapping his head off."

The little dog was scratching at the door, barking to the top of his lungs.

"I hear Judas," he said. "But there's other dogs. They're out in the swamp. They're barking up a storm."

Darlene strained to hear the other dogs.

"I can't hear a thing but that Judas," she said.

Ray opened the door and Judas scooted onto the porch. The little dog stopped at the top step, turned his face toward the swamp and started into his barking again. Ray had never heard such racket from Judas, not even when the mail truck was speeding down the hill from Gum Creek.

"Something's not right," Ray said. "I've heard the dogs barking before, when they're chasing a rabbit or a raccoon, or some other animal in the woods. But listen. They're not moving. They've stopped in one place."

"You *do* have good ears, Ray," Darlene said. "I hear the barking now, but I can't tell if they're moving or standing still."

"Something's not right, Darlene," Ray repeated. "Somebody's in trouble."

"But, Ray," she said. "How do you know....?"

"I just know. And we need to go, now."

Ray placed the cleaner and the paper towels on the porch table.

"Get 'em, Judas," he said.

The little dog sailed off the porch. He ran to the edge of the woods, stopped, and turned around and looked at Ray. He kept barking, turned around again, and shot into the woods.

"Let's go," Ray said. "Before Judas outruns us."

Ray reached out his hand and Darlene took it. Judas had entered the woods at a path that he and Ray had walked many times. Ray and Darlene followed the little dog. Within moments all three were swallowed up by the thick forest of Gum Swamp.

CHAPTER 23

Marie's eyes opened into thin slits. The canopy of big trees spun slowly above her. She wondered how long she had lain on the cool, damp floor of Gum Swamp. She squinted at her watch. A tiny crack ran across the crystal. The numbers wiggled like heat waves on pavement. She focused as best she could on the second hand. It wasn't moving.

Her leg throbbed, her head ached. She looked at the sky, barely visible through the veil of limbs and leaves. The sun was dimmer, lower in the sky than she had remembered it before the fall.

She shivered when she realized she had spent the night in the swamp.

"Marie, you crazy thing. What made you think you could do this? What made you believe this was going to be a simple walk in the swamp? Why are you always letting your curiosity get you in trouble? You're about as dumb as they come."

She heard a noise behind her, perhaps at the top of the ravine, the sound of someone or something walking among the leaves.

Her heart leaped.

Since her childhood, she had heard of the wild boars of Gum Swamp. A long time ago, in happier times, her father had related with great gusto tales of hunters who had encountered these fearless animals. Once, he told her, a man hunting alone spooked a herd of them. The wild pigs chased the man through the brambles and vines of the swamp, caught up with him, and gored him to death with their razor-sharp tusks. As a child, she had been frightened by this story, but as she grew older, she reasoned that her father had made up the tale, that he had told it to entertain her, or to keep her from traveling into the swamp.

But now, she believed it to be true. She believed wild boars were walking toward her, sniffing the ground with their snouts, turning leaves and soil with sharp tusks. How could she know that the animal at the top of the ravine was only a small bird, pecking at the cover of leaves, searching for something to eat?

Marie wept at the thought of wild boars, at the remembrance of her father, at her own foolishness. At that moment, her whole world seemed to be tumbling down a tall hill, rolling toward sure destruction, tumbling as she had tumbled into this wet and cold ravine.

She could not stop her tears.

They ran down her face and fell like small drops of rain on the forest floor. She thought then that she should pray. Deep within her soul, this simple idea blossomed into a strong desire. She resisted this urge to speak to God, to lay her problems in the lap of someone she believed had deserted her long ago, just as her own father had deserted her. She did not practice prayer. She had prayed many times in her life and could not remember a single answer. She had come to believe that prayer was for the weak, for people who needed some kind of crutch, some kind of imaginary arm to lift them out of the misery of living.

She did not count herself among the weak.

She thought of her mother, a woman who prayed often. Marie was twelve when her mother died. In those carefree days she and her family attended church. Her life was simple, sweet, full of promise.

She had allowed herself then to listen to the mysterious but certain call of God. She even thought she might one day be a missionary in a far off land. But her mother's death had changed all of this childish thinking. Marie had prayed that her mother would live, even when the doctors had given up hope. She told her father that God could heal anyone, that he could do anything he wanted to do. Despite her prayers, despite her hope beyond hope, Marie's mother had died. Seven years later, her Aunt Jeanette, a woman of great faith who had taken care of her after her father abandoned her, died of the same disease that had claimed her mother's vibrant life. When these strong women died, so did Marie's belief in a loving God who takes care of his children.

Marie tried again to squelch the notion to pray, but the idea would not leave her. She lifted her leg. A pain like an electric shock bolted through her leg and then the rest of her body. She gritted her teeth and fought in vain to hold back tears. She laid her hands on her face and moved her head from side to side. Damp leaves clung to her cheeks, her eyebrows, her lips.

"Oh, God!" she cried. "I can't take this any longer. I need help. I need a crutch. Please help me, Lord. Please help me. I'm scared. I'm dying. I'm too young to die. I'm not married yet. I just got my promotion at the post office. I'm lying in the middle of a swamp. My leg hurts. I can't move. I've lost my cell phone. Wild boars are coming for me. I need help. Please help me, Lord."

Marie cried harder. She tried to pray again, but she could not speak. She could not think. She sensed a strange trembling in her body. Her thoughts drifted like scraps of paper in the wind. She heard more noises in the forest, sounds of animals, of panthers or wolves or wild pigs or mad dogs foaming at the mouth. She could not focus on these sounds, for her thinking had become vapor, a fog floating among the branches of trees, a gray cloud hiding the light of day. Against the rising sun, she saw silhouettes of wild boars and snakes and her mother and father and Jesus. The images ran into each other and merged, forming a shadow, a film through which she could not see.

Then there was darkness.

CHAPTER 24

Good Lord," Darlene said. "It's a woman. She's hurt!"

"It's Marie Parker," Ray said.

"You know her?"

"Yes. She's the postmistress in Dogwood. Looks like her leg is broken."

Ray knelt beside Marie and placed his head on her chest. Judas was licking Marie's face and the other dogs, at least a dozen of them, were milling around, sniffing Marie's body, her camera bag, her cell phone.

"She's still breathing," Ray said. "But she's unconscious. We need to get her out of here. Quick, find a couple of stiff branches. We need to make a splint for her leg."

"But, Ray, I don't know how…. "

Ray stood and faced Darlene. He wiped a tear from her cheek with his finger. Her face relaxed.

"Darlene, it's OK," he said. "We need to just calm down a little. Marie's going to be all right. But we do need to get her out of these woods. I'll have to carry her out, but I can't move her until we get a splint on her leg. If we move her without the splint, the break will compound. We don't want that."

Darlene breathed deeply.

"OK," she said. "I'll be OK. You're right. We need to get her to your house."

"Now, you just stay here with her. Keep Judas and the other dogs from her face. I'm going to run back to the house and get some stuff for a splint. I'll call 9-1-1 while I'm there. Will you be OK by yourself for a few minutes?"

"Yes, Ray. I'll be OK. I just kinda lost it for a minute."

" Don't beat yourself up about it."

"OK."

Ray tore into the woods and Judas followed him. Darlene knelt beside Marie and brushed the hair from her face. She felt Marie's forehead and listened to her chest as Ray had done. She was relieved to hear Marie's strong heartbeat and to feel Marie's breath on her face. She saw that Ray was right about

Marie's leg. It was obviously broken, the bone pushing against the skin. She gathered Marie's cell phone and camera and bag. The other dogs had remained and she felt a degree of comfort in their presence. She looked around the forest and listened. She heard a train whistle in the distance and did not know if it was at the Petersboro Road crossing or at the other crossings Ray had mentioned. She wondered if Ray heard the whistle and she hoped he had not stopped to listen to it.

"What in the world are you doing out here?" Darlene said to Marie. "And how long have you been here?"

Darlene knelt beside Marie again. She held Marie's hand and was happy that it was warm. "Lord," she said. "This is the most unusual thing I think I've ever seen. But as strange as it is, this woman needs your help. I ask you, Lord, to touch her. Only you know why she's here. Only you know what happened. And only you can touch her spirit now, Lord. Help Ray and me to do what we need to do to help her. And heal her, Lord. And, Lord, help me not be so afraid of these dark woods. Amen."

Ray ran into the ravine. He was carrying an old sheet and two pieces of wooden dowel.

"Are you OK?" he said.

"Yeah. I'm good. And Marie's going to be good, too. The Lord's with us, Ray. He's going to make everything OK."

"I don't doubt that for a minute, Darlene. Now, let's do our part."

Ray ripped the old sheet into several wide pieces. He carefully placed the dowels on either side of Marie's broken leg. He wrapped the strips of cloth around the leg, tightening them with each wrap. He tied the strips together and straightened Marie's leg.

"Let's go," he said. "I called 9-1-1. They've got to come from Petersboro, and it'll take a few minutes. Hopefully they'll be here by the time we get to the house."

"Do you need help carrying her?" Darlene said.

"No," he said. "It'll be better if I just lift her myself. You walk beside me and make sure her leg doesn't strike a tree or a bush. Marty and Sherry are already at the house. I told them what happened and asked them to stay there and wait for the emergency people. And Rachel was just driving up."

"OK," Darlene said. "Let's get this poor woman out of here."

CHAPTER 25

Pastor Joseph Robbins had been thinking all day of the carvings.

He had received one and so had Zilphia Lassiter. Then, Jake Stanley's story appeared on the front page of the Dogwood Gazette, with photographs. The Stanley incident, as sensational as it was, was only the beginning of the story. Marvin Wilkins, Mary Della Johnson, and at least six others had reported receiving some kind of carving. All of the carvings were religious in nature, and all seemed to Pastor Robbins to have been very personal. Each person had stated to Editor Dudley that the carvings had come at just the right time, when they needed some kind of voice, some kind of sign, some kind of message from God.

It was one of the strangest things Joseph Robbins had ever witnessed.

And now the pastor found himself in his pulpit, trying to conduct a service, trying to begin his sermon, and all he could think of were the carvings, and his carving in particular; the preacher walking away from the little church. He straightened his stack of papers and read.

"Our text today is from Romans 3:23 'For all have sinned and come short of the glory of God.' Now, before we can apply this text to our lives, we must try to discover what the text is actually saying. We must ask ourselves what God really meant when he inspired the Apostle Paul to write these words."

Several of the Dogwood Community Church faithful shuffled in their pews. A few yawned. Others picked up their bulletins, eager to catch up on the church's activities for the week.

Pastor Robbins made a mental note of these distractions, as he did each week. He took a sip of water from the Dixie cup sitting on the shelf inside the podium. He coughed, not to clear his throat, but in a feeble attempt to regain the attention of his listeners.

"I believe we must try to know as much as we can about God and his purposes for our lives. When we do that, we begin to touch the eternal," he said.

A few more parishioners yawned.

As usual, he knew his sermon had already taken its first step on the road toward the dreary Village of Oblivion. He sensed that even these first few words had already become heavy shoes trudging through thick mud. But he kept reading. He knew enough about God's Word to trust that even if it is delivered in the most boring way possible it has a power all its own, a power to touch people's lives. In the case of Dogwood Community Church, however, the effect of the Word seemed to Pastor Robbins to be quite like the power of a good sleeping pill.

"We must first understand that the Greek word for sin is 'harmatia,' and if we look closely at this verse we will see it in its proper context. Harmatia literally means 'to miss the mark' as one would miss the bulls-eye in an archery contest."

Pastor Robbins kept his face toward the podium, his eyes on his notes. He continued in this manner until something in the back of the church ran across the corner of his vision. He was surprised to see Sammy Bender, a frequently absent member of Dogwood Community Church. Sammy had poked his head through one side of the double doors at the back of the sanctuary.

"Ahem," Pastor Robbins said. "As I was saying…"

Sammy whispered something to Miss Nora Adams, who was faithfully seated in "her" pew toward the rear. She looked back at him. He waved for her to join him, and she obliged without hesitation. Her hobbling around resulted in the dropping of a hymnal to the floor and the scattering of several papers, including a well-worn Sunday School quarterly and a church bulletin on which Miss Adams had sketched a drawing of her dog, Sparks.

Pastor Robbins ignored the intrusion as best he could, and continued with his reading.

"Now, imagine yourself as the archer, and the arrow as your life," he said. "You pull back on the bow, the arrow fletched and ready to fly. Then you let go of the bowstring and you are quite sure your arrow will hit the bull's eye. But, when it reaches the intended target, it suddenly veers and strikes far to the left or right or above or below the bull's eye, which is in the center, of course."

The commotion at the back of the church increased to a sort of low murmuring. Again, Pastor Robbins tried to pretend nothing was happening.

"This is how all of us are," he said, "Paul is telling us here that no matter how good an archer we think we are, we can never hit the center of the target—which is another way of describing true righteousness—without some kind of assistance."

A high-pitched shriek sliced through the sanctuary.

It was not a scream of fear or pain, but a cry of joy, of exuberance, of sheer exhilaration.

Pastor Robbins's first thought was that Wanda Dupree had come into the church without his notice. Wanda had always been quite spiritual, and had tried once to introduce a Pentecostal flavor to the Sunday services. She would mumble her own prayers while he was praying, raise her arms during the singing of hymns, and sometimes clap her hands during the choir special. She had been chastised by the chairman of the deacon board and then generally rebuffed by many other members. Finally, she stopped attending altogether. Pastor Robbins heard that she'd moved her membership to what some members of his church had called "that new holy-roller church in Petersboro."

This particular shriek, however, had not trumpeted from the lips of Wanda Dupree. It had blasted from the elderly lungs of Miss Nora Adams, who was—against all laws governing her age and physical condition—running down the aisle toward the pulpit.

"Pastor, Praise the Lord!"

A stunned Pastor Robbins could not respond.

"Praise the Lord! Sammy said he just got a call from Walt Nixon who got a call from Hazel at the diner who said that Chief Norris was about to head out to the hermit's house on Gum Swamp Road. He thinks the dogs are there, pastor. He thinks the hermit has stolen them and is using them in fights, with gambling and drinking and all other kinds of carrying on. Chief Norris is on his way there now. He's going to bring back my Sparks, preacher. Hallelujah!"

Miss Adams ran toward the door as quickly as her feeble legs would carry her. She held her cane in her hand, but did not use it as she danced up the aisle.

"But, Miss Adams!"

"Can't talk now, pastor. I'm riding with Sammy down to the hermit's house. I want to find my Sparks before he gets killed or injured in a fight. I just hope I'm not too late. Praise God from whom all blessings flow!"

Bob Jones and Mamie Wilson and her husband, Billy, all of whom had also reported dogs missing, joined Miss Adams in her frolic down the aisle. A handful of others decided they'd go along just out of curiosity.

"People!" Pastor Robbins said. "We must get back to the service. We've only just begun the sermon."

Pastor Robbins's words echoed off stained glass windows and faded to nothing. Within seconds the congregation, already pitiful in its numbers, had been reduced by half. Pastor Robbins gave the situation a moment or two of thought and turned toward choir director Jesamine Piner.

"Mrs. Piner," he said, with as much decorum as he could muster. "Would you kindly lead the choir in the benediction? Today's service is over."

Pastor Robbins gathered his sermon papers, placed them into his Bible, and stuffed the Bible under his arm. He walked out of the pulpit and toward the double doors at the back. He did not stop in his usual spot for the weekly shaking of hands. He walked down the 100-year-old brick steps of Dogwood Community Church, crossed the church parking lot, and stomped into the small patch of woods on the vacant lot on the other side of the street. A short distance inside the woods, he found an upturned plastic bucket. He sat on it and listened to the sound of tires crunching and tossing gravel on their way out of the church parking lot.

Pastor Robbins laid his Bible on the pine straw and leaves at his feet. He rested his elbows on his knees and plopped his chin in his hands. Never before had he been so angry with God's people.

A large crow, feathers shining like obsidian, perched in a tall pine tree above him. The bird cawed. The raspy, incessant noise sounded for all the world like a cruel kind of laughter. The pastor picked up a pine cone and tossed it at the crow. The huge bird refused to be intimidated by this feeble human effort.

"Get away! Shoo! Leave me alone!" Pastor Robbins said.

The crow stared at Pastor Robbins through cold, yellow eyes. The bird did not flinch a feather. Instead, it continued its dark, taunting, otherworldly laughter.

Pastor Robbins sat in his car. He bowed his head.

"Lord," he said. "I need a word from you. I don't know what to do. I don't know what else to say."

His cell phone rang.

"Hello," he said.

"Joe?"

"Yes. Oh, hi Karen."

"Joe Robbins, where in the world are you?"

"I'm here, at the church, sitting in my car."

"Where did you get off to? I was in the nursery and the next thing I know Amy Wendell comes in a half hour early to get Richie and tells me church is over. I went out there to see what was going on and you were nowhere to be found. What's going on, Joe?"

"Oh, nothing. And everything. I went across the street for a while."

"Across the street? There's nothing but a vacant wooded lot across the street."

"Exactly," Joe said.

"Well, I'm sure you'll explain everything once you get home."

"I will."

"Are you going to be OK till then?"

"Yeah, sweetheart. Thanks."

"OK. And by the way, Joe. Fred Lassiter called. Zilphia's not doing so well. The doctor says she probably won't last through the rest of the day. They want you to go over there."

Pastor Robbins realized then that Zilphia Lassiter was probably his only real friend, other than Karen, in the entire town of Dogwood.

"Joe. Are you there?"

"Yes. Yes, sweetheart. I'm here. Just didn't expect the news about Zilphia. She's been real sick. I guess it's not a shock, but I guess it is. I mean, sure, I'll go by there on my way home. I'm not sure when I'll get back to the house."

"That's OK. I understand. Are you going to be OK, Joe?"

"Sure. I'll see you later."

"Bye, sweetie."

Pastor Robbins closed the cover of his flip phone and laid it on the seat. Again, he bowed his head.

"Lord," he said. "Zilphia's the lucky one today. I'm sitting here feeling sorry for myself, thinking all I want to do is be in heaven, where you are. And Zilphia will most likely be there long before I will. Forgive my self-pity, Lord."

He backed his car from the parking space and made his turn onto Main Street. To his left, the large black crow kept its vigil in the tall pine tree on the wooded lot. The crow looked at Joe Robbins and cawed loud and long.

"That's it," Joe Robbins said. "Scream as loud as you want. I guarantee you won't get the last laugh today. Not by a long shot."

CHAPTER 26

Zilphia Lassiter lay on the bed her mother gave her when she and Fred were married. The bed belonged first to her great-grandmother, whose father had masterfully crafted it from an oak tree that had grown on the family farm. Zilphia promised the bed to her son, Frank, as a reward for his tireless efforts in researching the family's history, and because she loved him.

"If I could only feed her," said Fred Lassiter. "I think she might be OK for a while longer."

"Feeding her would not help, Mr. Lassiter," the hospice nurse said. "Her bodily functions have shut down. Food would be like poison to her."

Fred reached for a tissue on the table by the bed. He dabbed his eyes and turned his head so the nurse and his son and Pastor Robbins could not see him crying.

"It's OK, Fred," Pastor Robbins said. "This is something to cry about."

The doctor had been there an hour earlier. He told Fred that Zilphia would probably not survive until nightfall.

"The cancer has progressed so rapidly in the last few days," he said. "There is nothing we can do for her now, except the morphine."

That morning, Zilphia had been well enough to go downstairs for breakfast. She had not been hungry, but she ate a bit of the toast Fred prepared for her. Even then, Fred noticed her slurred speech and difficulty sitting up. After breakfast, she collapsed without warning on the dining room floor. Fred carried her upstairs and laid her on the bed and called the doctor. And now, Fred and Zilphia Lassiter were having the last conversation of their lives.

"You're going to be OK, Zilphia."

"Now, Fred, you know that's not true. You know as well as I do I'm dying. I've been dying for a long time."

"Don't talk like that Zilphy. Let's just forget this talk about dying. Let's get you comfortable on the bed. You can rest awhile. Doctor Bernard will be here soon and he'll give you something to make you feel better. Then you can rest all afternoon and I'll bring you supper in bed."

With great effort, Zilphia shook her head in disapproval.

"Fred, you need to understand something. I am really dying. This cancer has gotten the best of me. I've won a couple of battles for sure, but the cancer is winning the war. Accept it, honey. Just accept it."

"I don't know if I can, Zilphy."

"You can if you let the Lord lead you. He'll give you peace, Fred. He's already given it to me. And now I can already feel his arms around me. He's getting ready to carry me to heaven."

Zilphia coughed. Fred wiped her lips with a tissue.

"You see, sweetheart," she said. "Many times over the past few months I've questioned the Lord, doubted him, even gotten angry with him. Some days I'd be lost in my mind with worry about you and Frank and Josie and Little Frank. I could not understand how this could happen to me, how a God who loved me would let this happen. But now I see that I don't have to have all the answers, Fred, and neither do you. Through it all, the Lord never left me. He's always been faithful, even when I wasn't."

She coughed again and Fred bent over and placed his face against hers.

"I know you're right, Zilphy. Just forgive me for being human, for being sad about losing my girl."

Zilphia grabbed her husband's arm and pulled on it as best she could. He gave in to her tugging and kissed her on the face.

"It's been good, Fred. It's been very, very good. You're all I ever wanted and all I hoped you'd be. I have no regrets about marrying you, even though mother thought at first that you were worthless and no good. You sure proved her wrong."

Zilphia laughed weakly and Fred joined her on the bed. They lay there for a long time without saying anything. The nurse and Pastor Robbins and Frank understood the moment and left the room.

"Fred, go get me that plaque."

"Which plaque, Zilphy? You've got a dozen plaques. They're all over the house."

"The one with Romans 8:28 on it. The carved one with the vines and colorful flowers. I want to hold it and look at it."

Fred hurried down the stairs, found the plaque in the kitchen above the coffee maker where Zilphia had placed it on the day she found it, and brought it to her. She held it to her chest and hugged it tightly. She drifted into a very deep sleep. The people she loved most stood at her bed. Her husband and her son had been her entire life, and now they were by her side to witness her death. Pastor Robbins kept vigil by the window, his head bowed, his eyes closed. He tried to think of Zilphia and the kindness she had shown him. But all he could think about was the big black crow in the top of the pine tree on the vacant lot.

With his eyes, Fred caressed the face of his beloved wife. The room was as still as dawn. He could hear the clock ticking by the bed. Then, Zilphia Lassiter's eyes opened wide, as wide as Fred had ever seen them. Somehow he knew those eyes were seeing something beyond the walls of the bedroom, beyond the house, the street, even the clouds. Zilphia sat up in the bed and glanced around the room. The plaque slid off her lap and slapped the wooden floor.

"There He is!" Zilphia cried. "There He is! Praise His holy name!"

Pastor Robbins turned quickly toward his friend. His heart beat like a kettle drum in his chest. He shivered.

Then, as suddenly as she had risen, Zilphia slumped back onto her pillow. She closed her eyes. Her mouth froze into a slight smile. A quiet gurgle came from somewhere deep within her frail body. Zilphia Lassiter was gone.

Fred, sobbing, reached to the floor and picked up the plaque. He rubbed his fingers across the words, the flowers and vines. He placed the plaque on the bed by his wife. He crawled onto the bed and he laid his head on Zilphia's chest and his tears fell onto her bedshirt and onto the pillow and onto the beautiful wooden plaque.

CHAPTER 27

Marie thought she saw people silhouetted against a bright wall. The people were like trees waving in a breeze.

She remembered she was lying on the ground, on wet leaves, in a deep ravine in the heart of Gum Swamp. The throbbing in her leg reminded her she had been badly hurt. She knew she had been asleep, but she did not know how long.

"Now, sweetie, you take a sip of this water if you can. It'll make you feel better."

The voice was muffled, as though it had originated inside something hollow, like a jar or a bowl. Yet, it was soft, the voice of an angel. Marie's mind whirled. She knew then she had died, and that perhaps the angel was her mother.

The pain in her leg increased and it shook her, like strong hands, to awaken her. She could see clearly now. She realized she was not in heaven, but in a strange room, a room filled with strange people. She did not recognize anyone, except the man by the door. She had seen him before, though from a distance. Her mind reeled as she tried to place him. She felt her heart would jump from her chest when she knew with certainty that the man by the door was Ray Fulcher, the hermit.

Marie tried to sit up. She wanted to run, to leave this place. But the pain in her leg would not allow it. It was a hot pain, a boiling, and then a sharp tingling, like electricity. She understood then that the hermit had somehow discovered her in the swamp and that he had brought her into his house and tied her to his couch and was at that moment planning to do something horrible to her. She wanted to scream, but her mouth would not cooperate.

"There, girl, keep still as possible. You don't want to hurt that leg any more than you already have."

The voice was clear now. It was not an angel's voice, but a woman's. And the voice seemed sincere and truthful and caring. Marie relaxed, but only a bit.

"We've called 9-1-1, honey. An ambulance is on the way. You just take it easy and relax. You're going to be OK. You've had a nasty fall, that's all, and your leg is in terrible shape, maybe even broken. You got a little cut on your forehead and one on your right arm. But none of it is too serious. Praise the Lord for those dogs."

There was a sort of peace in the voice now, a heavenly kind of calm. She scanned the room. Her vision had cleared. In the room, four or five women mingled and talked. There were perhaps an equal number of men, also talking. Still, she recognized none of them, except the hermit. Her eyes met his and he smiled.

"Hey, Marie, nice to see you, though I do believe our first close encounter has been under somewhat unusual circumstances," he said.

Marie had never heard Ray Fulcher speak, and his voice was not at all as she supposed it might be. It was deep and resonate, like thunder that had been tamed and shaped. This voice, like the woman's before, carried with it an assurance that caught Marie off guard.

She moved her arms. She was not bound to the couch. Her mouth was not stuffed and gagged.

"I, er, I don't really know what happened," Marie said.

"Quiet now," the woman said. "You need to conserve your strength."

But Marie felt compelled to speak.

"I was walking in the swamp, looking for, uh, mushrooms, and I was getting hot and mosquitoes were biting and I had sort of lost my bearings, and I looked at my watch and next thing I knew I was on the ground in a sort of gully. I couldn't move my leg. I couldn't get up, I couldn't find my cell phone, and then I heard noises, and now I'm here, in your house."

Marie gasped for breath and coughed.

"Here, take some of this water," the woman said. "By the way, my name is Darlene."

Marie sipped the water. It cooled her throat. She had not realized how thirsty she was. She had never tasted water so sweet, so healing. She finished the glass and looked at Ray.

"You're, er, you're…"

"The old nasty hermit? Yes, I'm the hermit," he said, laughing. "And you're the postmistress. And you're in my house, lying on my couch, and my little dog Judas is watching you with a jealous eye because you're in his favorite spot."

Ray and Darlene laughed. Marie felt a grin grow across her face. Ray walked to the couch and knelt on the floor beside her. The last remnants of her fear melted when she heard him speak.

"Marie, you're going to be OK. Like Darlene said, the ambulance is coming. I believe your leg may be broken, possibly in a couple of spots, but there's no blood. The bone didn't break the skin. You'll probably be in a cast for a few weeks, but that'll work fine for you in your cushy new job as postmistress."

"But, uh. Mr. Fuclcher…"

"Please, I'm Ray. Just Ray."

"But, Ray, how did you find me?"

"It was the dogs, Marie. Darlene and I were sitting on the porch when we heard the dogs barking. Sometimes, they'll do that, you know, and usually it doesn't last long. They'll see a rabbit, or a tree will creak, or a car will turn around at the end of the road. They'll bark a couple of minutes and then hush. This time, though, they kept at it. Even Judas insisted on barking his little head off. So, we followed Judas after he took off through the woods. The other dogs had already gone into the swamp. I had a strange feeling about the whole mess, so Darlene and I just ran toward the barking."

"It was like a scene from "Lassie," Darlene said, chuckling.

"Well, the rest of the story is simple," Ray said. "The dogs led us to you. You were unconscious. I saw that your leg was most likely broken, so I left Darlene with you and ran back to the house for splints and a towel. We tore the towel and made a quick splint out of a couple of dowel rods and I picked you up, brought you here and called 9-1-1. We laid you on the couch and prayed for you, and you know the rest."

Marie wiped her tears with her dirty hands. Darlene offered her a soft bath cloth.

"Ray, Darlene, you rescued me."

"Don't give us any credit, Marie," Ray said. "It was the dogs, pure and simple. They found you. We just followed them to you."

Marie knew these must have been the same dogs that barked at her when she delivered Ray's mail. She thought of the stolen dogs, her conversation with Chief Norris, her reason for going into the swamp. Now she could not believe that Ray Fulcher, this man kneeling beside her, the man who carried her in his arms from Gum Swamp, who now seemed as kind as any man she'd ever known, was a dog thief, or any kind of thief, or even a hermit.

"I'm sorry, Ray," she said, dabbing here eyes with the cloth.

"Sorry? About what, Marie?"

"For thinking bad things about you."

Marie could not remember the last time she told anyone she was sorry for anything.

"Bad things? You mean, thinking I was an old ogre living in the swamp?"

"Not only that, Ray. You see, well, I don't know if I should tell you this, but…"

Marie turned her head into the soft cushions on the back of the couch.

"Tell me what, Marie?"

She looked at Ray and then at Darlene and then at Ray again.

"I didn't go into the swamp looking for mushrooms. I went to spy on you, to take pictures of your dogs and whatever else might incriminate you. I thought you were the one stealing those dogs in town. I was going to prove it, take some pictures. Now look at me. What a mess I've made."

Ray took Marie's hand.

"Don't worry about it," he said. "I don't mind people spying on me. I've got nothing to hide. And why would I want to steal dogs when they just show up at my doorstep on their own, usually without an invitation?"

"Amen to that," Darlene said.

"I don't blame people for thinking I'm some sort of hermit," Ray said. "I live beside the swamp. I drive a beat-up old truck. I keep to myself. And I'm not the most outgoing person in the world. I enjoy my solitude out here. I do get a little lonely at times, but I have my friends, and I have Judas, and Darlene."

"Notice I came last on the list, after Judas," Darlene said, laughing.

Ray winked at Darlene and smiled.

"It's just the way I want to live," Ray said. "A simple life, but one that suits me."

"I'm sorry," Marie said. "Really I am."

"All is forgiven," Ray said. "It's the least I can do for one of the Father's children."

He laid his hand on Marie's forehead and pushed back a lock of her hair.

"Now you just rest, Marie. Everything's going to be fine."

Marie closed her eyes again and thought of Ray's kind words.

"One of the Father's children" he had said.

Many years had passed since she had thought of herself as one of God's children. But now, lying on Ray Fulcher's couch, it made perfect and complete sense.

CHAPTER 28

Chief John Norris switched on the blue light as he turned his cruiser onto Gum Swamp Road.

His plan had, at first, been simple. He would approach Ray Fulcher with his concerns about the stolen dogs. He would listen and observe. If an arrest was warranted, he would do what he had to do.

But that simple plan flew out the window when he heard the county dispatcher radio for an ambulance at 4004 Gum Swamp Road, Ray's address. There was an injured person at Ray's house and this fact changed everything for Chief Norris. Professional curiosity exploded into urgency.

The cruiser kicked up dust as it barreled down the unpaved road. The trailing cloud lingered like fog, a fog thick enough to hide a small convoy of cars and trucks that had turned onto the road only seconds behind the cruiser. Chief Norris did not know about the excited tribe of Dogwoodians following him, all of whom had heard through the grapevine, and now on their scanners, that serious things were happening at Ray Fulcher's house.

Chief Norris sped past Elmer Tarkington's farm. Marie's truck was parked at the old tobacco barn. His instincts as an experienced law enforcement officer told him immediately that somehow Marie was involved in whatever was going on at Ray's house. There could be no other reason for the presence of her truck in such an odd place. He shook his head, switched on the cruiser's siren, and pushed a little harder on the accelerator. He fumbled under his seat for his pistol, found it, and laid it on the seat beside him. Because the headstrong Marie Parker was involved, he set his mind to expect the worst.

"Faster, Sammy," Miss Nora Adams said. Her voice cracked like baked rice cereal in milk.

"I can't go any faster, Miss Nora. I can hardly see a thing in this dust. It's just my luck we'd be going down the only unpaved road on this side of the county."

"The chief's turned on his siren, Sammy. My God, something bad is happening to Sparks. Hurry!"

Sammy Bender pulled his truck to a stop within a couple of feet of Chief Norris's cruiser. Miss Adams grabbed the dashboard to keep from crashing into it.

"Are you trying to kill me, young man?"

"Sorry, Miss Adams, the dust…. "

"Never mind. Let's just get out of here."

Sammy bounded from the truck and ran to Chief Norris.

"Chief! My dog! Thank you so much for helping me get my dog back. I knew when I heard the old hermit had stolen my dog it made sense. I just hope we got here in time, before he uses my poor, beautiful dog for God knows what. I don't know if I could take that…"

Chief Norris had been only a little surprised to see Sammy's truck and the other vehicles. He'd lived in Dogwood all his life and knew the tendrils of the small town's information grapevine reached far and wide. But what had begun as a simple attempt to satisfy his own curiosity had grown into serious police business. He did not need extra bodies in the mix.

"Whoa, Sammy," Chief Norris said, holding his hand up to Sammy's face. "You and the others need to back off. I'll handle this."

"But Chief…"

"I said back off, Sammy. And that goes for the rest of you."

The others had gotten out of their vehicles and were marching down Ray Fulcher's driveway. Only Miss Adams, exhausted from her jubilation at Dogwood Community Church and the rough ride down Gum Swamp Road, stayed behind in Sammy's truck.

"But Chief, listen. I hear dogs barking. One of them sounds like my Boo. The hermit's got my dog!"

The siren of the emergency ambulance echoed off Elmer Tarkington's house.

"Look people," he said. "This is a police matter now. Somebody's been injured and the ambulance is coming. Just step away and let me handle it. If your dogs are here, we'll find them. Just get in your cars and make way for that ambulance. Now!"

Sammy Bender and the others returned to their vehicles. They moved the vehicles onto the shoulders of the road, leaving just enough room for the ambulance to pass through. Chief Norris got back into his cruiser and drove down Ray Fulcher's driveway and parked at the side of the house. He was surprised to see a half dozen cars parked in the yard. The ambulance bounded down the driveway behind the cruiser and stopped at the front porch. Ray had already walked onto the porch and was waving the emergency medical people into his house.

"She's in here, on the couch."

Chief Norris followed the EMTs. There were at least a dozen strangers in Ray's living room. He was not surprised to see Marie lying on the couch.

"Marie, what happened? Ray? What's going on?"

"It's a long story Chief," Ray said. "I'll fill you in as soon as I'm sure Marie is OK."

"It's all right," Marie said. "Ray helped me. He and his friends saved my life."

"Saved your life? From what?" the chief said.

"Let's step out on the porch," Ray said. He grabbed Chief Norris's arm and led him to the back porch. He motioned for the chief to sit in the swing.

"What's going on Ray?"

Ray told the whole story. Chief Norris, taken a little aback by the improbability of it all, said nothing until Ray finished.

"I'll be darned," Chief Norris said. "That busy-body woman. Trying to spy on you. Getting lost in the swamp. I've never heard anything so…"

"Just a minute, Chief," Ray said. "Don't be so hard on Marie. She shouldn't have tried to spy on me. And she shouldn't have been in the swamp alone. But she's gone through a horrible ordeal. She spent the entire night out there, most of it unconscious. Her leg is broken, probably in a couple of places. Besides, she and I made up. We're buddies now."

"Buddies? How can you be her friend when she's done this to you and to herself, and to the rest of the people of Dogwood?"

"The rest of Dogwood?"

"Right now, there's a mob of angry folks sitting in their cars at the end of Gum Swamp Road. They think you stole their dogs, Ray. And Marie's the one who stirred everything up in the first place. I even let it get to me. I didn't come here because of the ambulance, Ray. I came here to see if you had stolen those dogs. I came to search your place. Marie had me believing all kinds of things about you."

Ray looked toward his barn

"Ray, have you heard a word I said? Ray?"

"Yes, uh, chief. I heard you. And I have an idea that just might fix this whole thing."

"At this point, I'm open to anything."

"Go back out front and tell all those kind people to meet me in about five minutes, in my back yard, out there by the barn. Tell them to come and get their dogs if they want them."

"Are you saying you stole their dogs?"

"No. That's not what I said. Just tell them to come to the barn. I'll take care of the rest."

Chief Norris stepped off the front porch. A sudden white light nearly blinded him. Instinctively, he reached for the place on his hip where he kept his holstered pistol. But he'd left the gun on the front seat of his cruiser.

"Mike! Get that camera out of my face!"

"Sorry, Chief," said the editor of the Dogwood Gazette. "It went off by accident. It's new and, well, I'm not used to it yet."

"Well, how about getting used to it out there in the yard and not in my face."

"Sorry," Mike Dudley said, letting the camera fall by its strap to his chest.

"Hey, Chief," Mike said. "What's going on? Seems to me the whole town is out here at the hermit's house."

"Not now, Mike," Chief Norris said, blinking rapidly, adjusting his eyes to normal light. "Later, when everything is settled."

"Settled? What has to be settled? What's going on, Chief?"

"Just trust me, Mike. You'll get your story. Just move so I can get back out to the road."

Chief Norris got back into his car, waited for the ambulance to drive away, then turned his cruiser around and drove the couple of hundred yards to the road. In a few minutes he returned. Close on his heels were several vehicles. The drivers parked in Ray's yard. Sammy Bender drove his truck over Ray's rose bushes. Miss Adams exited the truck first. She winced a little as a thorn from one of the rose bushes brushed against her leg. It did not slow her down.

"Chief, I've come for Sparks," she said. "I want my dog and I want that hermit arrested for thievery."

"Hold on, Miss Adams, and the rest of you too," Chief Norris said. "Come around with me to the back yard. If your dog is here, we'll find it. If Ray's the thief, he'll be arrested."

Chief Norris led the procession into Ray's back yard. The chief was impressed with the well-manicured grass, the tightly trimmed shrubbery, the orderly manner of Ray's flower beds.

"By the way, Chief. Who was that in the ambulance?" Sammy Bender said.

"It was Marie Parker."

"Marie Parker? That's strange."

"You don't know the half of it, Sammy," Chief Norris said.

CHAPTER 29

Ray stood by the barn. He grinned when he saw the procession of Dogwoodians, most of whom he knew only by name or by having seen them in town. He held a large plastic bucket. Judas sat at his heels, tongue and tail wagging in canine harmony. The little dog seemed keenly interested in the contents of the bucket.

"Is that the hermit?" Bill Jones said. "He sure don't look like no hermit to me."

"And what's a hermit supposed to look like, Bill?" Chief Norris asked.

"I don't really know," Bill said. "I just know that guy standing over there by the barn don't look like no hermit."

"Just follow me and hush," Chief Norris said. "Don't cause any trouble. Get your dogs, and go home, please."

Ray motioned for the crowd to join him at the barn. Chief Norris felt a bit intimidated by this twist in the situation. He thought that perhaps he had given Ray Fulcher too much leeway, that maybe this whole thing was a ploy of some kind. Maybe, just maybe, Marie was right about Ray. And maybe the hermit had injured her in some kind of altercation, and that he was the one lying after all. Besides, he did not like the looks of the dozen or so strangers he had seen in Ray's living room, all of whom were now watching the scenario from the screened back porch.

"All right, Ray," Chief Norris said. "What's the deal?"

"There isn't any deal," said Nora Adams, who hobbled up to Ray before Chief Norris could grab her. She pointed her cane at Ray's face and shook it.

"Look here, young man," she said. "What you've done is the most horrible thing I've ever heard of in my life. My dog is my best friend in this world and you've stolen him from me. When this thing is over, I hope they put you in jail and throw away the key."

Chief Norris grabbed Miss Adams by the shoulders and gently turned her toward the crowd.

"Don't be so hasty, Miss Adams. Let's let Mr. Fulcher have his say. If he's got your dog, he'll be duly arrested and tried in a court of law. I guarantee that."

"I don't want no guarantees," Miss Adams said. "I want my dog."

"Miss Adams," Ray said, a little shaken by the old lady's less than courteous display. "If your dog is here, you'll certainly get him back. I promise."

Ray poured the contents of the bucket into the three large aluminum bowls. The dry dog food sang its own catchy tune as it bounced against the metal. The dogs came then. They ran in from the swamp, from behind the barn, and from under Ray Fulcher's old pickup truck. They paid no heed to the crowd, diving through legs and across feet to get to the bowls. As usual, they found their places at the bowls and ate, with no fighting, no growling. And, as usual, Judas could not find a spot even tiny enough for his scrawny body to slide into.

"Don't worry, Judas," Ray said. "You'll get yours later."

The Dogwood mob stepped back and away from the food bowls.

"Now, Chief Norris," Ray said. "Here are my dogs. Well, they're not really mine. I don't know who they belong to. They just come and eat and hang around and…"

"OK, people," Chief Norris said. "There's one, two, three, four…. eleven dogs here, twelve counting the little strange-looking mutt. Get your pets and get out of here."

The Chief expected Miss Adams and Sammy Bender, and Bill Jones and the rest of the Dogwood folks to claim their dogs, but no one moved a muscle.

"That ain't my dog," Bill Jones said. "I'd know my dog anywhere. And that's not him. I'd never let my dog get so mangy looking."

"I don't see mine either," Sammy Bender said. "What did you do with my Boo, hermit?"

"Hang on Sammy," Chief Norris said. "Are you sure that's not Boo?"

"As sure as I'm standing here."

"Miss Adams. Do you see Sparks? What about that German shepherd there? Isn't that your dog?"

"Nope, and I'm ashamed of you, Chief Norris, thinking I would own a dog in that condition. Besides, Sparks has one straight-up ear and one floppy ear. I'd know him anywhere. He's my best friend. He's not here and I would be willing to bet my Chevy he's never been here. You, Mister Chief Norris, have led us on a wild goose or, I should say, a wild dog chase."

Chief Norris looked at the others.

"Well, what about it folks? Anyone see their dog here?"

No one spoke. They turned, almost in unison, and walked toward the driveway.

"Come on, people," Sammy Bender said. "The hermit doesn't have our dogs, unless he's already sold them, or had them killed in some fight somewhere. All he's got is these mangy, good-for-nothing mutts. There's not a pure-bred in the whole bunch, unless you count the fleas."

Sammy and the others walked to the front yard, got into their cars, and drove away. Chief Norris watched until the last vehicle was out of sight. He could not quite fathom the events of the last half hour.

"Well, Chief Norris," Ray said, chuckling. "I guess you've got the wrong man after all."

"Looks like it," Chief Norris said. "Look, Ray, I'm sorry about…."

"No harm done. Just another adventure, another example of one of life's great twists. I think it's wonderful how the Lord works things out. He has a purpose in all this you know. We just need to look around to see what it is."

Ray's remark about the Lord reminded Chief Norris of some of the things his wife says to him.

He doesn't understand it when Martha says those things, and he didn't understand Ray.

"Come on in the house, Chief. I've got some people I want you to meet."

The two men walked toward the house. Chief Norris could not place his finger on the source of the uncomfortable feeling in his gut until he made the first step onto the back porch stairs and turned around to look at the dogs gathered around the food bowls.

"Wait a minute, Ray," the Chief said. "There's something I didn't do."

"Something you didn't do? What do you mean, Chief?"

The chief pointed toward the dogs.

"Your barn, Ray," he said. I didn't search it. You know I'm gonna have to do that, don't you?"

Ray bent down and picked up Judas and scratched the little dog's head.

"My barn? There's nothing in there, chief, except some tools and a few odds and ends; some old motors and stuff. You don't need to check the barn. There's no dogs there."

Ray chuckled nervously.

"Sorry, Ray. But if I'm going to do my job thoroughly, I've got to search it."

Chief Norris stepped back onto the well-mown grass and walked toward Ray Fulcher's barn.

CHAPTER 30

Marie had never ridden in an ambulance. She'd never been in an accident, never been strapped to a gurney. She was surprised at the rough ride, the small jerks and jolts of the unpaved road, each one like a sharp knife jabbing into her leg.

"We're still on Gum Swamp Road, I guess," she said.

"Yes we are."

"I'm Marie."

"Mark. Glad to meet you."

"Where are you guys taking me?"

"Smith County Memorial. You've got a broken leg. Maybe in two places. They'll X-ray it at the hospital."

"I see."

"I heard you took a nasty fall down in the swamp."

"Yeah. Happened before I knew it. I tripped on something, maybe a root or a vine, hit my head hard, and passed out. I don't really remember much about the fall. I spent the night out there and didn't even realize it."

"You're lucky. I've always heard there were wild boars in that swamp. My dad told me not to go in there, that the boars would eat a person for supper."

"Yeah. I've heard those tales, too."

"Someone back there said you were looking for mushrooms, the edible kind."

"Well, I, uh, I suppose."

The ambulance driver pulled onto the paved highway and switched the siren on. Marie was thankful for the smoother ride. She was not happy with the noise.

"Do you guys have to run the siren?"

"Yeah," Mark said. "County policy."

"Even in a non-emergency?"

"Yeah. All the time, when there's a victim in the back."

Marie had not once during the whole ordeal considered herself a victim. If anyone was the victim in this mess, it was Ray Fulcher. She smiled a little when she thought of him. In that smile were mixed a dozen different emotions, all of which had been minimized somewhat by the fact that Marie was simply dog tired.

"Did you find any?" Mark asked.

"Any what?"

"Any mushrooms."

Marie's smile widened. "No. I didn't."

The driver slowed down at Brown's Crossroads. From there, Marie figured he would turn right onto State Highway 219, a straight shot into Petersboro, the county seat. She estimated she'd have another eight to ten minutes in the ambulance.

"But I did find something, Mark."

"I don't understand."

"You asked me if I found any mushrooms in the swamp. I'm just saying that I did find something out there, something much more important than mushrooms."

Marie could not believe what she was saying. She found herself praying again.

"What else is important in a swamp? Maybe buried treasure. My dad told me about the legends of buried gold in Gum Swamp. Made me want to go in there looking for it. Then the boar stories made me want to stay away. My English instructor at the community college would call that a paradox, or irony, or something like that."

Mark chuckled.

"Well, it wasn't exactly a buried treasure, though I guess you could call it that. What I discovered was I am still one of God's children, and that he does listen to my prayers, even when I've been far away from him for a long time."

She'd said it, and it had not been difficult at all.

"Oh, that kind of…I see," Mark said. He turned his attention from Marie to a white metal box attached to the side of the ambulance. A bold red cross was painted on the lid of the box. Mark opened the box and fumbled with the items inside.

"I believe it might be time to change some of these expired things in the kit," he said. "Don't want this stuff to get old and useless. Look, this eyewash is out of date, and so's the saline solution."

"I'm sorry Mark. I didn't mean to offend you."

"Not really, ma'am. I just don't, I mean, I don't go in for that kind of thing."

"What kind of thing, Mark?"

"You know, the God thing."

Marie prayed again, not aloud, but from somewhere deep inside. It was a strange prayer, not formed with words or ideas or requests or supplications, but made up of something much deeper than language.

"I know what you mean, Mark. The God thing is tough to fathom sometimes. I could write a book about it. But when I found myself out there in that swamp, helpless and in pain and not knowing what to do, well, I don't know, something deep within me urged me to call out to God."

"Yeah," Mark said, closing the lid on the first aid kit. He sat on the metal bench next to the gurney

"A lot of people do that when they need help," he said. "But when they don't need help and things are going great, they forget about God. I think it's kind of a crutch myself."

Mark's assessment sounded all too familiar to Marie. Yesterday, she had thought the same thing. But today was a new day for her. God, whoever and wherever he was, had listened to her cries of desperation as she lay hurt and lost in Gum Swamp. She was sure that he had seen her through the night without harm, and that he had sent a misunderstood man—with a pack of stray dogs—to help her.

"Crutches are good for people who need them," Marie said. "When I was lying on the floor of the swamp, hurting so bad I could hardly think, crying because I was lost, mad at myself for being so stupid, I needed a crutch. I was desperate. So I prayed. And, well, here I am."

Mark slid a little farther down the bench.

"Sorry, Mark. I guess I just talk too much."

"It's OK, ma'am. I hear lots of things back here. A lot of it I can't repeat. I hear what you're saying and, well I hope I don't offend you but I guess I'm not all that religious."

Marie considered the young man's remarks. He was "not all that religious," but neither was she. She had always seen religion as something people do, something that required a certain amount of public display, a following of rules, acting a certain way in a certain place at a certain time. A damp swamp swarming with mosquitoes, full of wild animals, teeming with mystery and danger was certainly not Marie's idea of a religious place. Yet, in the midst of that danger and mystery, she had experienced the presence of God. She knew she had learned a great truth about God, though that truth was as mysterious as the swamp in which she discovered it. And she could not yet speak that truth in words.

"I'm not religious either," she said.

Marie's words flew past the young man, who had turned his attention to the window in the back door of the ambulance.

"I'm sorry, ma'am," he said. "I was thinking about something else."

"What I'm saying, Mark, is that I'm like you. I'm not really all that religious either. But maybe, just maybe, that's really the best place to start with God."

Mark kept his eyes on the rear window. He watched the yellow lines of the highway fall away from the ambulance. He listened to the siren's hypnotic whine, and considered what Marie had said. He felt a strange stirring in his heart, but, like many times before, ignored it. He was glad when the ambulance finally pulled into the emergency entrance of Smith County Memorial.

CHAPTER 31

Chief John Norris rubbed his hand across the siding on Ray Fulcher's barn.

"Nice barn," he said. "This isn't pine."

"No," Ray said. "It's oak. Every piece of siding on this old barn is hand-sawn oak. Over 100 years old. When I moved here, I replaced eight pieces on the other side. Otherwise, it's original."

"They don't make 'em like they used to."

"It would cost a small fortune to build a barn of oak these days," Ray said.

"I guess so."

The two men stood silent for a while in front of the huge barn door. Ray placed Judas gently on the ground. The little dog trotted to the food bowls, which had been licked clean by the other dogs.

"Are you sure you want to search my barn?"

"Yeah, Ray. I'm sure."

"OK, but you're not going to find anything, at least not anything you expect to find."

Ray pulled the latch and swung the heavy door open. The ancient hinges creaked under the weight of the door.

"I like that sound," Ray said. "It's a sort of music to me."

Chief Norris chuckled. "Sounds to me like it's singing for a little oil."

Ray reached inside, fumbled for a switch, and flipped it. A rush of fluorescent light invaded the large, open room.

"After you, Chief."

Chief Norris stepped onto the concrete blocks in front of the door. He walked inside and was surprised that there were no dogs.

"No dogs here," he said.

"Just like I told you, Chief."

Chief Norris walked to the long workbench. On the bench were several hand tools; chisels, gouges, parting tools, drawknives, scorps, mallets. The tools were aligned perfectly on the table according to type and size. The Chief knew these were not the kinds of tools found in the average home improvement store. Their steel blades, their brass and wood handles, spoke of quality. He was not a woodworker, but he wanted to hold the tools, to use them in wood.

"I bought some of these old tools, "Ray said. "But my father left me most of them. He was an extraordinarily skilled craftsman, a luthier."

"Luthier?"

"Made guitars. Beautiful guitars. I have a couple of his instruments in the house, if you'd like to go see them."

"Maybe later. These are pretty nice tools."

The Chief stepped carefully, almost reverently. For a reason he could not explain, he sensed in his spirit that he'd stepped into a kind of sacred place. He was at a loss to understand it. Chief Norris moved his eyes from the workbench to the walls. On one wall, a dozen or more shelves housed pieces of wood; solid blocks, small and large, and cypress knees, barked and ready for carving. Some of the wood had been worked a little. Most of it stood blank, but inviting. On another wall, a series of box-like shelves rested. Inside each box sat a finished figurine. There was a dog that resembled little Judas, several other dogs of all sizes and shapes, a bear, an eagle, a beaver, all expertly crafted.

Because he was a professional law enforcement officer, Chief Norris tried to stifle the sense of wonder that had begun to stir inside him. It was a deep welling, a sort of awe, a spiritual feeling, something that made him edgy and comfortable at the same time. Then, like a lightning bug that surprises a child on a warm summer evening, a profound realization came to Chief Norris. He turned quickly to face Ray.

"Ray, you're the woodcarver."

Ray swallowed hard. He frowned. Then he smiled.

"Well, I do enjoy working with wood. It's something my father taught me and, well, I fiddle with it now and…"

"No," Chief Norris said. "I mean you're *the* woodcarver, the one who's been carving things for people in town. The one everyone's talking about."

"I didn't know people were talking about me," he said. "Except as a possible dog thief, and as an old hermit living out in the swamp."

Chief Norris laughed.

"I never would have guessed that you're the woodcarver, Ray. But, when I think about it, it makes perfect sense. Who else in town but that retired guy who lives in the woods of Gum Swamp would even have time to do all that carving? It's one of those fact-is-stranger-than-fiction things, like you see on TV."

The Chief walked to a shelf just beyond the workbench and picked up the carving of the small dog. He rubbed his palm against the wood, which had been sanded to a satin luster.

"Wait till the people in town hear about this."

"But, Chief, you can't tell them," Ray said. "You must not tell them."

"Not tell them? Ray, this'll make you famous, at least in Dogwood. Everyone in town is talking about the mysterious woodcarver who leaves figures and statues and plaques at people's doors, in their mailboxes, everywhere. Some people think it's Pastor Robbins, but he denies it, and rightly so. There was even a story in the paper."

"I know. I read that. Mike Dudley did a pretty good job of it."

"Why not tell, Ray? It certainly would clear up your image somewhat. Most people think you're an old man with a long scraggly beard who fights dogs and never takes a bath and who wanders through the swamp like some kind of witch or something. When they find out you're quite the craftsman, and a gentleman with great skill, those rumors will stop."

"You're probably right, Chief," Ray said. "But, you see, that's not what I want. I want to remain anonymous. I must. And I don't give a hoot about the rumors."

Ray stepped to the window on the side of the barn that faced his house. He waved at his friends, most of whom were still milling around on the back porch.

"You see those people up there?" Ray said.

"Yeah. They're strangers to me. But they look like nice folks."

"They're great folks, Chief. They're my closest friends and my brothers and sisters in Christ. I worship with them every Sunday. And that woman there in the blue jeans and the denim shirt with the embroidery on it. That's Darlene. We're kind of, well, seeing each other. And none of those people, not even Darlene, know what I do with my woodcarvings."

"Why, Ray? Why so secretive. Why not take advantage of the limelight? You could use a bit of positive PR."

"It's a matter of faith," Chief. "You see, when Jesus taught us about praying, he said that we should pray in secret, so that no one would see. He also said we should give our alms, our gifts, in secret, not letting our left hand know what our right hand is doing. I take the words of Jesus seriously. So, for me, the carvings that I do and that I give to others is like what Jesus was talking about. Carving is a gift that God has given me. He expects me to use it, not hide it under a bushel. But he also expects me not to glory in it. He should receive the glory, Chief, not me. That's why I keep it a secret. For me, it's a matter of faithfulness and obedience to my Lord."

"But Ray...."

"Please, Chief, please promise me you'll keep this a secret. Please say that you will never tell anyone I'm the woodcarver. I know you have to write a report of this incident, but could you keep out the details of what you found in my barn?"

Chief Norris placed the little wooden dog on the shelf and walked back to the workbench. On the bench lay another piece of carved wood. The carving was a man, like a prophet, standing on a rugged hill, a scroll in his hands. The man's mouth was open, as though speaking. The man seemed to be saying something very powerful.

"This is quite beautiful."

"That's just a little something I'm carving for Mike Dudley at the Gazette," Ray said. "I hope it will remind Mike that his writing talent is a gift from God, and that he should always use it to glorify the One who gave him that gift."

"But why don't you just tell that to Mike, Ray? With the carving, he might not get the message."

"Because I'm not a very good talker, Chief. I don't even *like* to talk. But I am very good at woodcarving. It's something the Lord has given me. I like to let Him speak for me, through my work, through the wood."

"He certainly does that, my friend, and he does it very clearly."

Ray switched off the light and closed the barn door. He walked the Chief to his cruiser. Mike Dudley stood by the rear of the car, waiting for the Chief's official report.

"If you've got a few minutes, I'll just take your statement and we'll be done, Chief," Mike said.

Chief Norris looked at Ray, then at Mike Dudley.

"Come by my office tomorrow, Mike. I'll write my report tonight and you can read it tomorrow. It'll have all the details in it."

"Can you give me just the gist of the story now, Chief? I mean, well, my deadline is noon tomorrow. If I could get started on the story tonight, I'd at least have my lead written and have some idea of a headline. It'll save me some time."

"OK, Mike, here's the nuts and bolts of the story. Ray Fulcher is not a dog thief. There are dogs here, for sure, but they're strays. No pure breeds. Not in the house, not in the woods, and certainly not in the barn."

Chief Norris winked at Ray.

"In fact, there's nothing in that old barn but an inch-thick layer of dust and a few lazy spiders."

"But what about Marie? What's her story?"

"Marie Parker came out to Gum Swamp to search for mushrooms. She got lost in the woods and fell down a ravine. She was knocked out and broke her leg and Ray's dogs found her and he and his friends brought her into his house and called 9-1-1. Simple as that, Mike. That's the meat of the story. Come by tomorrow and get the report."

Mike Dudley scribbled a few more lines in his notebook and placed his pen in his shirt pocket.

"Sure thing Chief. I'll see you then. Thanks."

Chief Norris and Ray watched Mike Dudley drive off. Within a few seconds, the dust from Gum Swamp Road swallowed the young editor's car

"Well, Ray, I guess that's it."

"Yeah, I guess so. Now, come inside and meet my friends. Get a glass of tea."

"I better get on back to town. Promised my wife I'd meet her at her mom's for lunch. Besides, I don't want to spend any more time out here in this dreary old swamp than I have to. Crazy place, Gum Swamp. Snakes and wild boars and mangy dogs and an old hermit who eats children for supper."

Both men were still laughing as Chief Norris drove away. Ray waved a final goodbye and walked back toward the house, to his friends who waited patiently inside. When he reached the steps, Judas was waiting, his tail wagging furiously.

"Well, good buddy," Ray said, picking up the little dog. "It's been quite a morning. If the Lord blesses me any more than he already has, I'll think I'll just pop."

Judas licked Ray in the face.

"Well now Judas, that's not exactly the kind of blessing I was talking about."

EPILOGUE

Robert Parker's fitful sleep was interrupted by a sharp pain in his left leg.

"You can't sleep here, old man. This is public property."

Robert opened his eyes. A large man was standing over him. The man wore a yellow hard hat and a bright orange vest over gray coveralls. "N.C. Department of Transportation" was embroidered in bright blue thread on the chest pocket of the coveralls.

"Huh?" Robert said.

"I said you can't sleep here. You gotta move on. This is DOT property. It's dangerous to even be here, and it's against the law."

"Oh," Robert said. "OK. I'll just be moving on then."

Robert had stopped at the huge culvert at sunset the night before. It seemed to be a good place to sleep. The culvert was dry and large enough not to be attractive to small rodents and other animals that might also choose to make it a home. He didn't have money for a motel room, so he had figured the culvert to be his best bet for the night.

"What you doing out here sleeping in a culvert anyway?" the DOT man said. "You don't have a home?"

Robert stood and brushed the loose dirt from his pants. He ran his fingers through his hair in an attempt to tidy himself up for the stranger. He stopped when he realized what he needed was more than tidying up.

"Well, I, uh, yes I do have a home," Robert said. "It's in Dogwood. My daughter lives there. I'm on my way—"

"Dogwood? You're a hundred miles from Dogwood. You going to walk all the way?"

"Yes," Robert said. "I don't have any kind of transportation, other than my own two feet. But they've served me well so far."

The man reached his hand toward Robert.

"Cramer," the man said. "Nathan Cramer."

Robert wiped his hand on his pants and took Nathan's hand.

"Robert Parker."

"Nice to meet you Robert. You seem like a decent guy. You don't have any weapons on you do you?"

"Weapons? Me? No sir," Robert said. "No need for weapons. Though I have been in a couple of situations over the last good while, situations where I could have used a stick or a baseball bat. But I don't carry any kinds of weapons."

"Hang on a minute, Robert," Nathan said. "Just stand right there. I need to make a quick call."

Nathan snapped his cell phone from its holster and punched in a couple of numbers.

"That's OK," Robert said. "I'll be moving on. No need to call anyone."

Nathan held his palm up to Robert's face.

"Like I said," Nathan said. "Just stand right there."

Robert picked up the dirty pillowcase that held all his earthly belongings. He looked to his left and then to his right, seeking the quickest possible route away from the steep embankment.

Nathan spoke into the phone. "Yeah, Billy. Nathan...Yeah, just checking on the culvert over hear at Mingo...Yeah. Look, I need to take an early lunch today...I know it's early, but I need to run some errands before this afternoon.... OK. I'll call you when I'm back in my truck...Sure. Thanks, Billy."

Nathan placed the phone in its holster. "OK, Robert," he said. "Looks like you're coming with me."

"But, I said I'd be going. I don't want any trouble. I just needed a place to sleep, that's all. I don't need to go to jail. That wouldn't be good—"

Nathan started the climb out of the embankment. He stopped about halfway to the highway and turned around.

"Well, are you coming or not?" he said.

"I'll be OK," Robert said. "I'll just hit the road and you won't have any more trouble out of me."

"But you're not going to hit the road, Robert," Nathan said. "You're coming with me. And I'm bigger than you and I can make you come with me if I have to."

Nathan smiled.

"OK, I'll come," Robert said. "Looks like I don't have a choice."

"That's right," Nathan said. "Now come on up here and get in my truck."

Robert followed Nathan up the embankment. Nathan opened the passenger door and Robert slid into the seat.

"Just push those tools aside," Nathan said. "Skinny as you are, you shouldn't have any trouble finding room to sit."

Nathan laughed. Robert did not understand the big man's jovial mood. Nathan walked to his side of the truck and got in.

"I just need to ask you one thing," Robert said.

"And what's that?"

"Where are you taking me?"

Nathan started the truck, checked the side mirror, and pulled onto the highway.

"A little place I think you'll like," Nathan said.

"The county jail?"

"No, not the jail," Nathan said.

"Where then?" Robert said. "I think I have a right to know where you're taking me."

"My house."

"Your house? Wait a minute. You're not some kind of pervert are you?"

Nathan's laugh boomed and filled the truck. Robert flinched and Nathan laughed again.

"I come along and find you sleeping in a culvert," Nathan said. "You're filthy and need a bath worse than my dog does. You stink and your clothes look like they've come from a dumpster. It's obvious you haven't eaten much in a while. Your beard is scraggly and your breath smells like a trash truck. And you think *I'm* the pervert? That's rich, Robert. Really rich."

Nathan laughed again and Robert forced a smile.

"There you go," Nathan said. "By the time me and Edna are done with you, you'll be smiling for real. Me, a pervert? Wait till I tell that to Edna. She'll get a kick out of that for sure."

"Some people bring home stray animals. Nathan brings home stray people."

Edna placed the bowl of mashed potatoes on the table. She sat and Nathan said a prayer of thanks for the food.

"Now, Robert," Edna said. "Dig in."

"I wouldn't place people in the same category as dogs," Nathan said. "But I guess it's the same principal."

He laughed and covered his roll with a chunk of butter.

"Edna's used to it by now," Nathan said. "In fact, I believe she rather enjoys helping folks out. We both see it as a kind of Good Samaritan thing. It's something we can do for the Lord."

"I am grateful," Robert said. "I'll have to admit I was thinking at first that you might turn me in to the authorities."

"He wouldn't do that," Edna said. "Unless he thought you were dangerous."

"I've had a couple of run-ins with folks who weren't as nice as you, Robert," Nathan said. "Those, I let the sheriff handle. I'm not going to take any risks. But I had a feeling about you. That's why I brought you here."

"Thank you," Robert said. "It was good to take a bath, put on clean clothes. Though yours are not what I would call snug."

Nathan laughed. "I've been telling Edna that maybe I should go to the thrift store and get a set or two of smaller clothes, just for folks like you. See what I mean, Edna. My clothes swallow Robert up like he's in a cave or something."

Edna snickered. "But clean is clean," she said.

"Yes," Robert said. "Clean feels good."

"You'd be amazed at the folks I run into working for DOT," Nathan said. "But not everybody wants to take advantage of our hospitality."

"I can't imagine why they wouldn't," Robert said.

"Picked up a guy two weeks ago. He was sleeping in the woods in the interchange on I-95 over by Taylorsville. I convinced him to get into the truck. He smelled worse than you, Robert."

"I can't imagine that either," Robert said. He laughed and it felt good.

"Well," Nathan said. "We were driving along, not saying anything and when I stopped at the intersection at Creech's Crossroads, he just jumped out of the truck and hightailed it into the woods. I knew I couldn't run as fast as him, so I just closed the passenger door and drove on."

"The Lord didn't want that one in our house," Edna said. "No telling what kind of trouble he might have caused us."

"You're probably right, Edna," Nathan said.

"No probably about it," she said.

Robert took a bite of fried chicken and sipped his iced tea. He and Nathan and Edna were quiet for a few minutes. The aroma of good food and the cleanliness of Nathan and Edna's home reminded Robert of Gertrude's boarding house.

"So," Nathan said. "You're heading to Dogwood. To see your daughter."

"Yes, um, Dogwood," Robert said.

"Some daughter," Edna said. "Letting her daddy live outside like an animal."

"It's not like that, Edna," Robert said. "It's, well, it's a long story."

Nathan reached for another roll.

"Now Edna," he said. "We agreed we wouldn't judge."

"Sorry," Edna said. "It's just that, well, I get curious about some of the folks Nathan brings here.

Sometimes they talk and sometimes, most of the time, they don't. Like you, Robert. Most seem to have something they want to hide or something that's just too painful for them to talk about."

"Edna," Nathan said. He gave his wife a hard look.

"No, Nathan, that's OK," Robert said. "It's just that, well, I haven't seen my daughter in twenty years, and it's my fault, not hers. I've been trying to get back to Dogwood to face her. But, I don't know, I just can't seem to get the courage to do it.... It's just a long story."

Robert could not believe that he was telling these things to strangers. But, for some reason he could not explain, he saw Nathan and Edna as old friends, though he'd only known them for an hour. He felt at home in their house, at ease at their table. But now, the thoughts of facing Marie brought back the same old fears. He did not want to say any more about it.

"More tea, Robert?" Edna said.

"Yes, please."

Edna got up from the table and went into the kitchen. She returned and placed the glass by Robert's plate.

"So, Robert," she said. "What's it like, being on the road, I mean? Seems to me it would be a great adventure."

Robert looked at Nathan and Nathan turned his head to his plate and scooped a spoonful of mashed potatoes to his mouth.

"No, not an adventure," he said. "Mostly hardship. Just a few days ago, three guys came up to me in the train yard at Fayetteville."

"Oh, Fayetteville," Edna said. "I have a sister in Fayetteville—"

"Edna," Nathan said, his voice slightly muffled by the mashed potatoes.

"Oh, sorry," she said. "Go ahead, Robert. I didn't mean to interrupt."

"It's OK, Edna," he said. "Well, the three men wanted to rob me, but when they saw I didn't own anything worth robbing, they got mad and just beat me up right there in broad daylight. One of them hit me on the head and I blacked out. I awoke in the emergency room at the hospital—"

"My sister works in the hospital."

Nathan shot Edna another hard look. He rolled his eyes and pursed his lips together.

"Oh," she said. "What in the world happened next?"

"The doctor treated me, said it wasn't serious. Then a police officer, I guess he was the one who found me and brought me to the hospital, he took me to the city limits and told me not to come back to Fayetteville or else I might have to spend time in jail."

"Oh, my," Edna said. "I guess being out on the road's not such a good adventure after all."

"No," Robert said. "Not at all."

Nathan pulled his truck off the highway and into the parking area at the BP station. Robert read the sign on the other side of the parking lot at King Road. "Welcome to Dogwood, Town of Friendly Folks." The sign had not been there twenty years ago. Neither had the BP station.

"You sure this is as far as you want to go?" Nathan said. "I can take you all the way to the house, if you want."

"No, Nathan, you've done enough already," Robert said. "I can't begin to thank you enough for what you and Edna have done. The bath and the clothes and the food and taking time off work to drive me all this way—"

"Don't worry about it," Nathan said. "The Lord sent you our way today. It was meant to be. But, I'd be glad to take you to your daughter's house."

"Frankly, Nathan, I don't know if she even lives here any more," Robert said. "A lot can happen in twenty years."

"You're right. Twenty years is a long time," Nathan said. "But I have a good feeling about it. I think it's all going to work out for you and, what'd you say her name was?"

"Marie," Robert said.

"Yeah, for you and Marie. Who knows, you might have a son-in-law by now and a handful of grandchildren. You never know."

"That would be something," Robert said.

The two men sat in the truck for awhile. Neither of them spoke for what seemed an eternity to Robert.

"I guess this is good-bye then," Robert said. He pulled the door latch and Nathan placed his hand on Robert's shoulder.

"Hang on a minute," Nathan said. "I want to pray with you before you go."

"Pray? Well, I guess that would be OK."

Nathan kept his hand on Robert's shoulder. He cleared his throat. "Lord," he said. "Thank you for bringing Robert our way today. Give him strength and watch over him. I don't know what's in his heart right now, but I guess he's just plain scared. Take away his fear. And protect him, Lord. Amen."

"Amen," Robert said. He pushed the door open and stepped onto the pavement of the BP parking lot. He turned to Nathan. "Thanks, Nathan," he said. "And say thanks to Edna for me. Maybe our paths will cross again."

Nathan smiled. "For some reason, I think that just might happen, friend," he said. "You've got our number. Edna put it in the bag with the food. Call us if you need us. I mean that."

"I know you do," Robert said. "No doubt."

He closed the door and backed away from the truck. Nathan shot up his hand and Robert waved in response and then Nathan's bright yellow DOT truck pulled away from the BP station and back onto the Petersboro Road. Robert watched until the truck was out of sight. Then he breathed deeply and wondered what he would do next.

Sherwood Lassiter arrived first and unlocked the door and turned on the lights. Martha Norris came next, and then James and Irene Furman, Godfrey Lewis, and Mary Cashwell.

"Where's that old man of yours?" Sherwood asked Mary.

"Had to work," Mary said. "He wanted to be here."

Sherwood threw his hand toward Martha. She grabbed his hand and shook it.

"How's John doing?" he said. "That dog case was something, wasn't it?"

"Yes, it was," Martha said. "You know John. Once he gets his mind on his police work, it's hard to get him to think about anything else."

"Except his chickens," said James, laughing.

"Yeah, he loves his chickens. Sometimes I think he loves them more than me," said Martha, laughing now with James.

"You know that's not so," said Irene.

Everyone laughed. Then the small room was quiet for a minute or two. Godfrey Lewis stirred in his chair and it squeaked like old wooden-slat chairs are supposed to squeak. A bell clanged and the gates at the Main Street crossing fell. The southbound Amtrak car-train whizzed through town and was gone in seconds. Godfrey checked his watch.

"Folks heading to Florida," he said.

Martha coughed to clear her throat.

"Well," she said. "I guess we all know why we're here tonight."

"To pray, I hope," said Mary Cashwell.

"Yes," Martha said.

"We need it," Sherwood said.

"Amen," said James and Irene in unison.

"The Lord has just placed it on my heart that we need to pray for our church," Martha said. "I don't know what has happened to us in the last few years, but things have gone downhill a lot. We need to pray that the Lord will help us revive our church."

"It's all the arguments we've had," Godfrey said, nervously. "I mean, how can the Lord do his work in a church that's always fighting about something. Seems to me like that's not the Lord's work, but the Devil's."

"The Devil don't work in people who won't let him work in them," James said.

Martha wrung her hands and Godfrey shuffled his feet and Irene took a tissue from her purse and dabbed it to her eyes.

"We need to pray," Martha said. "I know this is a small group, but big things can come from a small group. Big things can come from just one person if they're doing the Lord's will."

"Amen," said Godfrey.

Martha stood up and closed the door. A small wooden sign clapped against the door. The sign announced that this room hosted the James J. Parker Memorial Men's Sunday School Class.

She sat down and waited. She wanted one of the men to take the lead, to begin the prayer. The air conditioning unit came on outside the window.

"Sherwood, you're the chairman of our deacon board," Martha said. "Would you begin our prayer for us?"

"Yes. Yes I will," Sherwood said.

They reached for each other's hands.

Sherwood asked the Lord for guidance. He said he was at a loss as to how Dogwood Community Church could continue to function without some kind of change. "What do you want us to do, Lord?" he said. "What do you want me to do?"

Martha spoke softly. "Lord," she said. "I feel the same as Sherwood, and all the rest of the people in this room. We need you to come to us like you did in the book of Acts, Lord, like a rushing, mighty wind. Send your Spirit, Lord. All of us in this room feel that our pastor is going to be leaving us soon. We don't blame him, Father. He's tried his best to help us. Who are you going to send to us, to lead us? I don't even know how to pray what I'm thinking tonight. The words just don't seem to come. But you know what's in my heart, Lord. We just need some help here at our church. Help us. Lord, help us."

Irene cried. James put his arm around her shoulder and pulled her closer to him. Godfrey shuffled his feet again and Mary sniffed a couple of times. Irene reached into her purse with her eyes still closed and retrieved a tissue and gave it to Mary. No one said a word for a long while. It was a good pause, a powerful kind of waiting. The crossing gate bell clanged again and a train's whistle blew a long and low moan. It was the northbound freight. The locomotive inched its way through the crossing and the engineer switched gears in anticipation of the long, gradual slope toward Lake Hansen.. The whistle moaned again, low and long. Martha waited for the clickety-clack of the train's wheels against the rails to stop. It seemed to take forever. Then, the room was quiet again.

"Lord, we don't know what else to say tonight," Martha said. "But you know what's in our hearts. You know the concern and love we have for your church here in Dogwood. Please help us, Lord. Amen."

The others echoed with amens of their own.

Sherwood stood first. Irene held her hand out for Mary's tissue and then she tossed hers and Mary's into the small metal trashcan by the door. Godfrey's left foot caught a chair leg and he almost tripped. James still had one arm around Irene's shoulder, but he threw out the other to catch Godfrey.

"My goodness," Mary said.

"Sorry," Godfrey said. "I'm OK."

"That last train, it was Bill Warren's train," Sherwood said. "We roomed together at State. He lives up in Waldensburg. He was on the sidetrack down at Juniper Road, waiting for the Amtrak to go through.

He does that long, low whistle to say hello to me sometimes. Sorry if it bothered anyone."

"Didn't bother me," James said. "It was somehow appropriate."

"Yeah," Godfrey said. "Like maybe the Lord was telling us something. That maybe he's going to help us. I don't know. But that's how I felt when I heard the whistle."

Sherwood pulled hard on the door. It jammed at the top and he jerked it hard. "I've been meaning to plane that door down some," he said.

"Thanks for coming tonight," Martha said. "I know you all are busy, just like everyone else. But I believe the Lord will honor our prayers. He's going to do something good here in our church. I just know it."

"Amen," Sherwood said. "We just gotta believe it."

Sherwood was the last to leave. He turned the lock on the doorknob at the rear entrance to the Sunday School hall, glanced down the hall one last time, and flipped the lights off. He closed the door and jiggled it to make sure it was locked. He walked across the parking lot, and stood by his car. He heard Bill Warren's train whistle again as the engine approached the Petersboro Road crossing at Lake Hansen, four miles away. He smiled and looked into the night sky.

"Thank you, Lord," he said. "Thank you."

Pastor Robbins laid his robe carefully on the old quilt in the trunk of his car. He glanced around the garage and closed the trunk. He had never liked funerals and had occasionally been criticized by members of the congregation, many of whom thought his funerals were too short.

"You can't cover a person's whole life in twenty minutes," Nora Adams told him after the funeral of her old friend, Melba Johnson. "You didn't even read a poem. When it's my time to go, I want you to pad things a little, keep them in the pews for at least half an hour. It's only right, you know."

But today was different. Zilphia Lassiter's passing had been a difficult thing for Pastor Robbins to accept. She was his favorite parishioner, his friend, a truly Christ-like person whose faith in the Lord inspired even a doubter like him. He was going to miss his weekly meetings with Zilphia. He was going to miss their friendship.

He walked into the kitchen and his wife held the phone out to him.

"It's Russell, your old friend from seminary," she said.

"Russell? I haven't heard from him in years."

"Something must have happened," Karen Robbins said.

"Hello, Russell? Is it really you?"

Karen Robbins did not like that she could hear only her husband's side of the conversation.

"Yes, fine, well I guess it's fine. Long story. How about you?"

Pastor Robbins turned toward the refrigerator, hiding his face from his wife, as though this would keep her from hearing what she could not hear anyway.

"Me? Why did you think of me?"

"What, Joseph? What?" Karen whispered.

He held up his hand in an effort to hush her. He listened intently to his friend.

"South America? Well, I don't know, Russell, that's a long way. And the kids are in school and, well, I don't know. We're pretty comfortable here."

Karen Robbins saw an immediate change in the familiar face of the man she loved. His lips tightened and his brow crunched. She could think only the worst.

"Comfort zone? What do you mean? Well, I guess I never really thought of it that way."

Karen eased to her husband's side and strained to hear the voice on the other end of the line. But she heard only jabbering. Pastor Robbins sat in a chair by the refrigerator. He listened for a few more minutes. Karen watched as her husband's face relaxed.

"You know, Russell, I can't see any real reason why we couldn't. To be honest, things aren't going so well for me here. In fact, I'm in the deepest rut of my life. I've been praying and talking to Karen and.... well, I guess...OK, then Russell...I know it's a risk...sort of like standing on the lip of a waterfall...Never mind, I'll explain later. No, I don't believe I need time to think about it. When a door opens, and I mean really opens, we must walk through it, right? OK. Call me tomorrow and we'll work it out."

Pastor Robbins gave the phone to his wife. She hung it in its place on the wall.

"Work what out, Joseph?" Karen said, returning to face her husband. For the first time in many months, Karen could see that her husband was beaming.

"What, Joseph? Tell me what's going on?"

Pastor Robbins placed his hands on his wife's shoulders and looked into her eyes.

"Karen," he said. "I love you very much."

"I love you, too, Joseph. Now, tell me what that phone call was about."

"Brace yourself."

"Brace myself for what?"

"Karen, we're going to South America!"

Chief John Norris waved for Hazel to re-fill his coffee cup.

"It's sealed, Boyd."

"What's sealed?" asked Boyd, his head buried in the newspaper.

"That last word. S-E-A-L-E-D. Sealed."

"Oh man, I wasn't even that far yet. I was only on the second one. I would have gotten an easy word like that."

"I know that, Boyd. You're about the smartest man I know." Chief Norris laughed hard. Everyone in the small restaurant looked his way to see what was so funny.

"You're hilarious," Boyd said. "You sure know how to embarrass a guy."

"I think it's impossible for you to be embarrassed, my friend."

"You're probably right. Hey, speaking of embarrassed, I saw the story in the Gazette. Seems like the hermit embarrassed all you guys out there the

other day. I guess he wasn't the mean old dognapper after all."

"No, Boyd, he wasn't."

"I sure would like to have been a fly on the wall,
watching all you folks out there. Or instead of a fly
on the wall, how about a flea on a dog?"

Boyd laughed at himself.

"Well, Mike Dudley got a few of the facts a little
mixed up, but they were minor mistakes," Chief
Norris said. "Miss Adams didn't flail at me with her
walking stick, nor did the ambulance driver get stuck
in Ray Fulcher's front yard. I don't know where he
came up with those tidbits. But the rest of the story
is pretty factual."

Boyd didn't respond. He'd already turned his
attention to the fourth word in the Jumble.

"That's it," he said. "Canine. C-A-N-I-N-E.
Funny. We were talking about the dognapper and
the next word's canine. Ain't that funny?"

"Yeah, hilarious," said Chief Norris, over the lip
of his coffee cup.

"By the way, John, didn't I hear you say earlier
that they finally figured out who was stealing all
the dogs?"

"Yeah, Boyd. Got the news this morning. It was
a gang of folks up in Wright County, just below the
Virginia line. They were coming south as far as Fayetteville, stealing dogs from about a six-county area.

They'd take them back up to Wright and have dog fights on Friday and Saturday nights. The Wright County sheriff broke them up just this past weekend. Found probably a hundred or more dogs, some of them in real bad shape. Ransom Wallace was the one stealing the dogs in Dogwood. You remember Ransom, don't you Boyd?"

"Sure, John. Who can forget Ransom Wallace? I'm not surprised."

Boyd scribbled something in the margin of the newspaper.

"By the way, John, any of Dogwood's missing canines among the ones they found in Wright County?"

Boyd seemed proud to have used a Jumble word in a sentence.

"We don't know yet. The vets are checking them all out, then folks are going to be allowed to go up there and claim their dogs, if they can prove ownership."

"What if no one claims them?"

"I guess they'll adopt them out, or put them to sleep."

"Maybe Ray Fulcher could go up there and get him a couple more dogs," Boyd said, laughing. "They'd fit right in with his mangy mutts."

Chief Norris didn't laugh at his old friend's remark.

"Hey Boyd, I've got an idea." he said.

"And what's that?"

"Finish your Jumble, and take a sip of coffee. That just might close that mouth of yours for a few precious seconds."

"What'd I say?"

"Never mind, Boyd. Just never mind."

Marie placed the phone on the receiver. It was the second time that day that Jim Barnes had called her. He'd offered to come over and help her tidy up the house, wash the dishes, pick her up for work, whatever she needed. She thought it was sweet of him to be so nice, especially since she'd been so cold to him at the store.

The thought of another date with Jim crossed her mind. She liked the idea.

She hobbled to her bed, propped the crutches against the wall by her nightstand, and, balancing as best she could on one foot, laid herself onto the bed. She exhaled deeply, wincing from the sharp pain this simple movement brought to her leg then to the rest of her body.

"Eight more weeks of this. I think it'll drive me crazy."

She reached for the old Bible on the nightstand. She had found it only today, inside the bench at the piano. She had placed it there years ago, on a day she could not remember.

She made herself as comfortable as she could on the bed, then opened the Bible, beginning at the first page. Tears came to her eyes as she read an inscription, in handwriting that she recognized immediately as her mother's.

"My Dear Marie. Now that you have discovered for yourself the wonderful love and salvation of our precious Lord, my prayer is that you will discover, in this book, His book, the wisdom and power of His Word. He loves you so much, Marie, and you are His special child. With all my love, Mom, your sister in Christ."

Marie lingered on the inscription for awhile, remembering things she had not thought of in many years. Her years in Sunday School, her mother's strong hand holding her own hand as they walked to church, simple songs of childhood. She laid the open Bible on her chest, reached for a tissue in the box on the nightstand, held the old book again. She tried to read through her tears, fumbling the pages. A photograph fell from the Bible. She laid the Bible by her side and picked up the photograph, knowing before she looked at it that it was a picture of her mother and father, standing beside the old Ford her father had been so proud to own. Between these two handsome and strong adults stood a child, little Marie Parker, seven years old. In the photo, Marie wore a frilly dress and new shoes. Her hair formed a pony tail, adorned with several ribbons. It was an Easter Sunday morning and the world was fine and correct and the way it was supposed to be. She held the picture in her trembling hands and wondered if her world would ever again contain the joy of that one Easter morning so long ago. And then she felt a strength in her heart, a rush of quiet peace, a reassuring sense that seemed to pierce the very marrow of her bones. Yes, somehow, the Father would come through for her, as he did not many days ago as she wrestled with her pain—physical and spiritual—on the cool, damp floor of Gum Swamp.

In the silence of that high-ceiling bedroom in the old house on the corner of Main and Stanley streets, in the small town of Dogwood, Marie Parker received a whisper from God himself. "I am your true Father. And, in time, you will see your earthly father again. And after all is done, all the people in that photograph will reunite for all eternity."

Marie could not contain her tears as the unspoken words poured into her mind. And in the midst of the tears, she spoke, and her words were a prayer.

"Father, you have rescued me and brought me back into your love. I believe the words you have just spoken to me. I believe them! And I give you praise and thanks and ask you, Lord, to lead me in the path you have cleared for me. Thank you, Father. Thank you!"

On the other side of Dogwood, at the end of a long, unpaved road, behind a house hidden among the oaks, maples, gums, and cypresses of Gum Swamp, Ray Fulcher opened his barn door. He switched on the light, made sure Judas was inside, closed the door, and sat on the stool at his workbench. Judas took his usual place on the old piece of shag carpet beneath Ray's feet and laid his small body down, resting his head on his front paws.

Ray held a piece of cypress in one hand and a chisel in the other.

"You know, Judas," he said. "I love this old chisel. It was my dad's. They don't make them like this anymore. It just plain old feels good in my hand. Solid, you know, real solid."

He placed the chisel on the wood and pushed. The chisel bit. He'd worked on this particular carving for a couple of days, and now it was beginning to take shape. It was an angel, one of Ray's favorite subjects. The angel's wings were spread, as though in flight. Hair, long and flowing, fell back across the angel's wings. In one hand, the angel held a trumpet to her mouth. In the other hand, a scroll of parchment. In one corner of the parchment, Ray had carved a postage stamp. On the parchment, he had carved these words: "You are my child. I love you."

"Judas, this one's for Marie," Ray said. "She needs to know just how much her Father loves her. I think she'll like the postage stamp. Don't you?"

Judas wagged his tail.

As Ray carved, small chips of wood fell on the head of the little dog. But he didn't move from his carpet. He did not consider the wood chips a nuisance, and made no effort to avoid them. Judas saw them not as residue or as the mere leftovers of the work of an artist, but as small drops of love, raining down on him from his Master.

To order additional copies of

THE
HERMIT
OF
DOGWOOD

Have your credit card ready and call:

1-877-421-READ (7323)

or please visit our web site at
www.pleasantword.com

Also available at:
www.amazon.com
and
www.barnesandnoble.com

Watch for publication of

The Book of Dogwood, Book II
in the Dogwood series by Calvin R. Edgerton.

Visit the author's website at calvinedgerton.com.

Chatham County Libraries
500 N. 2nd Avenue
Siler City, North Carolina 27344

Printed in the United States
57772LVS00001B/48